The Masked Gun

Also by Barry Cord
in Large Print:

Cain Basin
The Deadly Amigos
Gallows Ghost
The Gun-Shy Kid
The Guns of Hammer
Hell in Paradise Valley
Last Chance at Devil's Canyon
The Long Wire
Six Bullets Left
Slade
Gun Junction
Two Graves for a Gunman

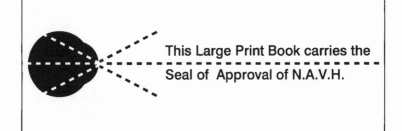

This Large Print Book carries the
Seal of Approval of N.A.V.H.

The Masked Gun

Barry Cord

WHEELER
PUBLISHING

Published in 2003 by arrangement with Golden West Literary
Agency.

Wheeler Large Print Western.

The text of this Large Print edition is unabridged.
Other aspects of the book may vary from the original edition.

Set in 16 pt. Plantin.

Printed in the United States on permanent paper.

Library of Congress Cataloging-in-Publication Data

Cord, Barry, 1913–
    The masked gun / Barry Cord.
      p. cm.
    ISBN 1-58724-521-3 (lg. print : sc : alk. paper)
    1. Sheriffs — Fiction.   2. Outlaws — Fiction.
  3. Large type books.   I. Title.
PS3505.O6646M37 2003
    813'.54—dc22   2003058053

The Masked Gun

As the Founder/CEO of NAVH, the only national health agency solely devoted to those who, although not totally blind, have an eye disease which could lead to serious visual impairment, I am pleased to recognize Thorndike Press★ as one of the leading publishers in the large print field.

Founded in 1954 in San Francisco to prepare large print textbooks for partially seeing children, NAVH became the pioneer and standard setting agency in the preparation of large type.

Today, those publishers who meet our standards carry the prestigious "Seal of Approval" indicating high quality large print. We are delighted that Thorndike Press is one of the publishers whose titles meet these standards. We are also pleased to recognize the significant contribution Thorndike Press is making in this important and growing field.

Lorraine H. Marchi, L.H.D.
Founder/CEO
NAVH

★ Thorndike Press encompasses the following imprints: Thorndike, Wheeler, Walker and Large Print Press.

CAST OF CHARACTERS

Ben Codine

He roamed a savage land in search of the man who made him an outlaw.

Ira Flint

The wolf who disguised himself as the wolf-hunter.

The Kansas Kid

He saw his death in the stars.

Jake Grady

The money he planned to give away might seal his doom.

Aline Buskin

As a schoolteacher, she unintentionally taught Ben Codine a lesson.

Travis Paine

To serve crime, he played the role of a marshal.

I

Fire rimmed the western hills as the sun sank down behind them. In the quick-flowing dusk fringing the creek Ira Flint's bitter voice flung its challenge: "Give me a gun, Codine! One bullet! You owe me that much!"

The tall man standing by Ira's horse ignored him. He made a motion with his hand and the outlaw looked down at him for a moment, his eyes dark and bitter and hating. Then the pent-up breath went out of him in a slow sigh; he dismounted, awkwardly because his wrists were handcuffed behind him. He stood facing Codine, sullen-mouthed, waiting.

Ben Codine said: "Turn around." His voice was flat and expressionless. But Ira moved. Codine unlocked one wristband and shoved Flint toward a sapling growing by the edge of the stream. He waited while Ira turned, his back to the slender trunk, then he stepped behind him, passed the dangling cuff around the tree and locked it around Ira's wrist again.

Ira turned his head and watched Ben walk back to his big black horse and start to loosen the straps holding his warbag. Codine was a tall, rangy man with a shuffling walk like an Indian's, quiet and balanced and

9

deadly. His hair grew long down his neck, shaggy and curling slightly. It was brown, flecked with red when the sun hit it right. His eyes were gray; they lightened or darkened with his mood, but they were always level, cold and quietly disconcerting.

He was a man in his early thirties. A strange man, he drifted across the frontier like a shadow. He was a searching man, a man searching for something he had once owned and had lost and was not sure he would find again . . . a woman, a home, roots. There was that brooding quality in the man.

Flint watched him with the cold regard of a wolf eyeing its captor. They were camped in the middle of nowhere, on a flat plain that appeared untenanted as far as he could see. The outlaw fretted silently as Ben Codine went about making a small campfire. His gaze reached out into the gathering darkness behind the bounty hunter. He searched the shadows along the creek for a long moment before turning his attention back to Codine.

"Pretty down-at-the-heels outfit," he taunted. "Bounty hunting doesn't seem to pay off, does it, Ben?"

Codine shrugged. "It's a living," he said, and turned away from Ira.

"What'll they give you for me?"

Codine frowned. He reached inside his saddlebag and took out a folded dodger and read it again. "A thousand dollars." He turned and studied Ira now, a small interest gathering in his eyes. "They want you real bad in King City."

"Bad enough," Ira admitted.

Codine shrugged and started for the creek with the coffee pot. Ira said after him: "Bad enough to hang me!"

Codine paused and looked back at his prisoner. "I reckon you deserve it," he said bleakly. "But hanging you isn't my job — nor judging you."

Ira Flint ducked his head down to meet his hunched shoulder and scrunched his Stetson back off his forehead. Standing, he was as tall as Ben Codine and as wide through the shoulders. Except that he had tawny hair, bluish-gray eyes and an insolent, ruthless cast of features, he might have passed for Ben Codine.

"An even break," he taunted harshly. "You're a legend out here — the great Ben Codine! They say even Wild Bill side-stepped a showdown with you!" His laughter rang arrogantly in the dusk. "Give me a chance to see just how fast you really are —"

"You're a fool!" Ben cut him off coldly.

"I'm better with a gun than you are!" Flint snarled. "I wouldn't be here now if my horse hadn't stepped in a chuck hole and thrown me!"

Codine studied the man briefly. He had

run down many men since the day he had buried his wife and five-month-old son, most of them with well-earned reputations as killers. But this big fellow he had cuffed to that tree was as dangerous as a leashed tiger. There was a prowling deadliness about Ira Flint that made him, barely in his mid-twenties, one of the most wanted outlaws west of the Missouri.

There was little doubt that Flint would be hanged once Ben brought him in to King City. His trial had taken place a year ago, and his sentence passed. A bribed deputy had offered an avenue of escape two days before the hanging and Ira had made it safely into Mexico. He might have remained there, despite efforts at extradition. But he had deliberately chosen to ride north again, across the Mexican border. Ben had run him down right after Ira held up a stage out of El Paso, run him down and captured him without a fight.

Perhaps it was just as well, Ben thought. He did not want to kill any man, unless forced into it.

The sunset glow was dying behind the hills. The flat prairie lay in darkness. Below him the shallow pool under the cutbank reflected the bright aquamarine streak of sky. Ben turned his thoughts away from Ira and studied the steep bank, looking for a way down to that quiet pool.

The small fire he had built flickered his

long shadow across the narrow river bed. In the darkness of the grove behind Flint, Ben's big black stallion, Nig, and Ira's dun-gray mare moved restlessly.

It was a peaceful evening. Somewhere in the soft dusk an owl hooted querulously.

The sound touched Codine's consciousness and slid away. Flint's harsh, demanding voice overrode it. "Give me an even break, Ben! A gun in my holster, a split second to prove I'm the better man!"

"You'll be dead!" Ben snapped. "It won't prove anything to you then!"

The tawny-haired outlaw shrugged. "And you save the state a hanging. What have you to lose? You still get your money. Unless —" his sneer was broad and baiting — "unless the great Ben Codine is afraid!"

The bounty hunter turned away. He was too old a hand on the trail to let Ira nettle him into a play like that.

He took two steps along the river bank, searching for a way down. The owlhoot made its thin, lonely sound again and now something warned Ben, a sense of danger as intangible and yet as definite as a passing shadow.

But the shot came before he moved. He felt the smash of the rifle slug in his chest, knocking him sidewise. He fell off the cutbank, into a well of darkness. . . .

Ira Flint waited impatiently, rattling his

cuffs against the sapling. The echoes of that single shot faded into the stillness. Only Ben's campfire made its small, crackling sounds.

Finally a shadow moved out of the darkness fringing the creek; it moved at a cautious lope toward the fire.

"I thought you'd never get here!" Ira snapped.

The shadow emerged into the firelight. He was a small, oldish man a foot shorter than Ira. Narrow as a bed slat and as wiry and tough as a bedspring. Nondescript range clothes hung loosely on his frame. The face that turned toward Flint was seamed and impassive and stained with dribbles of tobacco juice at the mouth corners. A pair of faded blue eyes surveyed the manacled outlaw with cool, shrewd regard. He spat slowly into the dust by the fire.

"I got here as soon as I could," he said finally. "I heard you shooting yore fool mouth off, Ira. Good thing Codine didn't take you up on it."

Flint sneered. "He wasn't that good, Wally." Then with raw arrogance: "He *couldn't* be!"

The smaller man turned away, shaking his head. He walked to the river bank and stood looking down at the sprawled figure lying with right arm and shoulder in the still pool.

A night bird made a dark pass over Ben's body and faded into the brush. A prowling coyote paused on a low sandhill a hundred yards away. He caught the scent of man and melted into the darkness.

"Hated to do it this way, Ben," the small man muttered. "To a man like you."

"Hell with that, Wally!" Ira snarled. "He's got the key to these cuffs in his pocket. Get me free!"

The ambusher slid down the crumbly bank and crouched beside Codine. He set his rifle aside and used both hands to turn the big man over, and it was then that he noticed the slight rise and fall of Ben's chest. He reached for his rifle, levered a shell into place, then paused as his narrowing gaze explored the blood-rimmed hole at the edge of Ben's shirt pocket. The sharp fear that had quickened his breathing faded. Hell, the man was as good as dead.

He found the handcuff keys in Ben's trouser pocket and climbed back up the bank.

"He's still alive," he said as he freed the tawny killer. He said it casually, his attitude neutral.

Flint rubbed his chafed wrists. Then he walked to the edge of the river and looked down at Ben Codine. Ben's upturned face was a white blur in the darkness.

Wally came up and stood beside him, slanting the muzzle of his Winchester down at the still figure. "Best to finish the job," he said. His voice was dry and without feeling.

"No!" Flint's hand shoved the Winchester barrel aside in rough gesture.

Wally eyed him with cold puzzlement. "He might fool us and pull through."

Flint's laughter had a cruel edge. "We're sixteen miles from the nearest town. Far as I know there's nothing inbetween. If Ben Codine's man enough to beat these odds, let him!"

"He'll come after us!" the older man warned. There was doubt in his voice, the thin edge of fear. "Wherever we go, he'll come after us, Ira!"

Flint's laughter was as wild as the wind off the far hills, and as unfettered. "Maybe that's what I want, Wally! If Ben pulls through this — and he doesn't have the chance of a snowball in hell — I'm going to give him reason to come after us. Because starting right now I'm going to give this country the worst damn scare it's ever had! I'm going to give them Ben Codine *turned outlaw!*"

Wally's eyes were wide. "You've gone loco?"

"Maybe," Ira grinned bleakly. His eyes were on the distant hills, as if he saw his future rise darkly against them. "I'm a gambler, Wally, always have been. I find no fun in the sure thing. It's not winning the big pot that matters; it's bucking the odds that gives a zest to living!"

"And a quick way to dying!" Wally muttered

harshly. He brought his rifle muzzle around again. "I still say we ought to make sure!"

Ira shook his head. He slid down the embankment and crouched beside Codine and went through the bounty hunter's clothes. When he scrambled back up the bank he was holding Ben's wallet, and he was wearing Ben's cartridge belt with the big Peacemaker nestling in the scuffed holster.

His voice had its old cocky insolence as he shoved the wallet into his pocket. "Ride with me, Wally, and watch me shake Texas from the Panhandle to the Mexican Border!"

He turned to the fire and kicked it out, scuffing sand over the embers. Then he crossed to the picketed horses in the shadow of the grove.

Ben's big black stallion jerked at his picket line, not liking this tall stranger. He was waiting for Ben; there was that sort of closeness between them.

Wally held the big black horse while Ira flung Ben's saddle over him, tightened the cinch strap and mounted. The outlaw waited impatiently for Wally to saddle the bay mare and join him. They rode to the creek bank. Below them Ben Codine had not moved.

Ira Flint thumbed his hat back rakishly on his head. "From now on I'm Ben Codine," he said. "Just one more touch will complete the picture, some black root dye for my hair."

Wally stared sullenly at him. "You're crazy," he muttered. But there was a grudging admiration in his tone. He looked down at the man sprawled below them.

"Let me finish him —"

Flint cut him off. "He's a dying man. Sixteen miles out of nowhere, without a horse, without a gun. He'll be dead before morning!"

"Just the same —" Wally began stubbornly.

"He's got one chance in a million," Flint sneered. "That's the way fate stacked the deck. Not even the devil himself can buck those odds!"

Wally shrugged. "Reckon yo're right," he said. But he looked back once as they rode away. And the lingering doubt in him remained.

II

A cool breeze ruffled the waters of the small pool, tugged at Ben's hair. A night bird tittered in the oak grove. The sound caught the ears of a prowling coyote. Silent as a drifting shadow, the four-footed prowler moved toward the grove. He came along the creek bank and then the faint movement by the pool below him froze him; he became a gray shadow among the deeper shadows.

Questing eyes studied the movement, judging it with a hungry scavenger's quick appraisal. The long dark figure rolled over and began bunching up. Water made its thin drip of sound in the stillness.

Disappointed, the coyote turned and melted into the night.

Ben Codine remained on his hands and knees, fighting the burning pain in his chest which threatened to black him out again. He was hurt badly; he knew this through the fuzziness in his head, which made thinking an effort in slow motion. The bleeding was not bad. But as he tried to stand he felt the warm blood ooze out and trickle down his chest.

He staggered and put an arm against the cold bank of earth and held himself erect. He listened. They were gone; he sensed that. And he knew, too, from a look at the star-hung sky that he had been unconscious a long time.

They must have thought him dead — Flint and the man who had shot him. Strangely, through the burning pain, a grim clarity worked inside the bounty hunter. He remembered now the short, slat-thin oldster who had been standing on the corner in Creosote, the last town he and Ira had ridden through. A tobacco-chewing harmless-looking old coot who had glanced at Ben and his prisoner, wiped his mouth with the back of his hand and turned away.

A little gesture, remembered now too late.

There was no time for regret. The iron will of the big man thrust through this momentary feeling of bitterness and settled with implacable tenacity to the problem of staying alive.

Ira Flint had made one irrevocable mistake. He should have finished Ben Codine when he had the opportunity.

It took most of Ben's strength to gain the top of the stream bank. He sank to his knees and put one hand on the ground to steady himself; he could feel the blood pumping out of the hole in his chest. Reason forced him to take notice of this now. He found his handkerchief and wadded it against the bullet hole, holding it hard against the flow with his left hand.

Bit by bit his iron will forced strength back into his quivering muscles.

He straightened, searched the dark grove for sign of motion. He knew Ira was gone, but he clung to the improbable hope that his horse, Nig, might have broken away. It was a vain hope. He whistled once, the high note breaking off on his stiff lips. Only the night wind answered him, and then, the far off, doleful yipping of a coyote. He turned then to the grim task of finding someone in this emptiness before his strength ran out; before even his stubborn will had to bow to the inevitable.

It was too far back to the town he and Ira Flint had last come through. He had only one slim chance — that somewhere along this small creek snaking across the dark plain some squatter had built his shack.

Grimly, he started to follow it.

The morning sun lifted against the curtain of dark hills and rode the shadows of night away. A pinkish glow bathed the land; it touched Ben's pinched face. He lay sprawled on the ground, his face turned to the sun. It was the sixth time he had fallen . . . or the seventh. He had lost count.

There was no strength left in him. A great lassitude weighed him; a small voice inside him nagged at him to quit this senseless striving, this blind movement that brought only pain and the bitter taste of defeat.

He lay still, gathering the last trickles of strength from the remote recesses of his body; his bitter will goaded him. He had to try *just once more!*

He forced himself up to his feet and turned with glazed eyes toward the sun. He was moving away from the creek, but he didn't know it. He moved toward the warming sun, like a moth toward a candle flame. And then, faintly, he heard a dog barking.

He kept walking, each stride shorter, more dragging. He saw the dog then, as through a red gauzy haze, a small, wire-haired terrier running to meet him. Behind the dog, in the far wavering distance was a small child with golden curls, chasing after it.

Ben took three more steps before his will cracked; he didn't feel the hard impact of the ground.

The dog ran around him, sniffing at his motionless figure. The girl came up and stopped and stared with wide blue eyes. She was five years old. Then she turned and ran back to the 'dobe and pole shack by the creek, and as she ran she cried: "Mommy! Mommy!"

The woman who came out at her cry was tall, fair-headed, wearing a gray apron over homespun. She was young, but work and worry had traced their age lines in her face and dimmed the youthful glow in her eyes.

She called sharply: "Cynthia! What's gotten into you?"

"A man, Mommy, a man over there." The child turned and pointed. "He fell down . . . he hurt himself, Mommy."

Fear flashed into Alice Hope's eyes. She turned and ran inside the cabin and emerged with a shotgun. Her husband, John, was on his way to town. She and Cynthia were alone here, but she had a frontier woman's hard capability.

She followed Cynthia back to Ben Codine. It didn't take more than a cursory examination to assure her that the man lying in the dust posed no threat to her. In fact, she wondered if he were not dead. She could detect no sign of breathing. Then she saw his hand move, saw him begin a blind, impossible effort to lift himself to his feet. There was no strength in him, but he kept trying!

She tried to lift him. She was a tall woman and hard work had toughened her. She raised Ben's head and shoulders and started to drag him toward the house, but she had to quit after a dozen yards. She stared helplessly.

John had left an hour ago; it would be late afternoon before he returned.

She was bending over Ben again when she heard the faint halloo. Startled, she turned and shouldered the shotgun. And then a thankful sigh escaped her.

It was her husband, returning with the wagon. She waved and waited for him, her smile edged with relief as he rolled up, a heavy-shouldered, sun-darkened man with light gray eyes under bushy blond brows.

"Forgot that letter to the mail order house," he said apologetically, then, glancing down at Ben's unconscious figure, he scowled. "Trouble?"

She shook her head. "Cynthia found him a few minutes ago. He's been shot. I think . . . I think he's dead."

The man stepped down from the buckboard and bent over Ben, placing his ear against his chest. "Not yet," he muttered, straightening. "Might even be a chance to save him." He frowned. "Wouldn't let a dog die without trying to help him," he said gently. "Least we can do for him is try."

His wife nodded. Together they managed to get Ben into the wagon and over to the 'dobe house. They carried him inside, laid him down on the home-made bed.

"You fetch the doctor," Alice urged her husband. "I'll do what I can for him until you get back."

She went to the door with her husband, watched him climb back into the wagon. "And hurry," she added softly, and watched him drive away.

When he first examined Ben Codine, Doctor Millar, a balding, thin man from Creosote, gave the bounty hunter no chance at all. Two days later, with frowning amazement, he gave Ben a fifty-fifty chance to live. Ten days later he brought a bottle of Irish whiskey and split it with Ben and John Hope in sober celebration.

"I didn't give you a chance in hell," he admitted to Ben. "Medically speaking, you shouldn't be alive."

Ben grinned wryly. "I'll remember that, when I come to town to settle my bill."

It was three weeks later before he was able to do that.

What he owed the Hopes he knew he could never repay with money. Alice Hope's unstinting, tender care, more than the doctor's visits, hastened his recovery. A stranger in their house, they gave him what they had and asked nothing in return, not even who he was.

To little Cynthia he became "Uncle Ben," which was as much of himself as he gave to them.

He did not tell them who he was. Only that he had been waylaid and robbed, stripped of money and saddle horse and guns.

He did not tell them who he was because he made a grim discovery the second week of his convalescence. It was in a paper brought back from Creosote by John Hope. The *Creosote Gazette* ran an interesting box item, reprinted from the *San Antonio Times*. The news item said that Ben Codine, bounty hunter, had turned outlaw — had traded on his reputation to rob the Wells Fargo Express Bank at Mineola. Codine had been positively identified by witnesses who described the big bounty hunter with the Peacemaker Colt, riding a big black stallion.

Additional items began cropping up in the *Creosote Gazette* until they made headlines. BOUNTY HUNTER STRIKES AGAIN: HOLDS UP CRACK SANTE FE EXPRESS AT DALEYSVILLE. . . . BEN CODINE HOLDS UP BANK IN DAWSON. . . . CODINE AND GANG WRECK TOWN OF RED BUTTE. . . .

There were a few indignant reports from citizens who didn't believe the news stories, loyal friends who tried hard to refute the incredible facts reported by apparently sincere eyewitnesses.

Sheriff Bill Tolliver of Rawhide, Texas was the only friend Ben could really rely on. He was his brother-in-law. His blunt statement, quoted in the *Gazette*, brought a small, grateful smile to Ben's lips:

". . . *I'll believe Ben Codine has turned outlaw when I see him face to face . . .*"

Five weeks from the evening he was shot, Ben Codine was ready to ride again. The Hopes were poor folks, but they lent him a horse more used to the plough than a saddle to ride to town. Ben said he'd leave it at the livery for John to pick up later; they believed him.

There was a telegraph office in Creosote. Ben wrote a message to Sheriff Tolliver; he signed it Ben. Handing it to the telegrapher he said: "Send it collect. I'll wait for an answer."

He got it that afternoon. There were two wires. One was addressed to Frank Stover of the Creosote National Bank; it directed Stover to give the bearer of this telegram $100 in cash and to loan him whatever amount he might need for the purchase of a horse and saddle. A wire of credit from the President of the Rawhide Bank accompanied it. The other, to Ben, simply stated: *Glad to hear you're alive. Will be expecting you at rendezvous.*

Ben paid Doctor Millar and then left all but twenty dollars with the livery man for John Hope.

Three days later Codine rode down into a draw on the outskirts of Rawhide and pulled up by a small shack.

Sheriff Tolliver was waiting for him. They shook hands.

"You look a little pale, Ben." His brother-in-law's voice held his concern.

Ben's eyes held a far-away, thoughtful look. "You brought what I asked for?"

The sheriff waved to a trim roan mare with an intelligent gleam in her eyes. "She isn't Nig," he said. "But she'll take you where you want to go, Ben."

The bounty hunter nodded. He followed the sheriff into the shack and Tolliver handed him a gunbelt with a walnut-handled Colt snugged in holster. And a sealed envelope which Ben slid down into his pocket. Money from his account in Rawhide. He had his savings in a joint account with Bill Tolliver. Bill and his wife and children were the only family he had, now that his wife and child were dead.

Bill watched Codine heft the Colt, get the feel of the gun, its balance. "How'd it happen?" he asked.

Ben told him, sparing no detail, yet with no embellishments. Tolliver frowned.

"Ira must have thought you dead and saw a way to trade on it. From what you say, he could easily pass himself off for you, if he dyed his hair."

"He's got Nig," Ben said grimly. "Where was he last heard from, Bill?"

"He was headed north," Tolliver growled.

Ben held out his hand. "Thanks for everything, Bill. I'll be traveling —"

"You still look a bit peaked," Bill protested. "Stay awhile. Lucy and the children. . . ." He made a gesture with his hands. "Hell, we hardly get a chance to see you, Ben!"

Ben said: "You told them?"

"I told Lucy," Bill answered. "I had to. . . ." He took a breath. "Made her feel easier."

Ben nodded. "I'll be back . . . someday."

Tolliver went to the door with him and watched Ben mount the roan mare. A great weight had been lifted from his shoulders when he had received Ben's wire, but now as he watched that grim figure lift a hand in farewell misgivings flooded him. A short half prayer came to his lips as he waved back:

"*Vaya con Dios*, Ben."

III

Against the pale background of snow the mining town of Labelle made a dark, sprawling blotch, spreading across the curve of the river. East of town, rails made their pattern, arrow-straight across the flats, fading into the early winter afternoon grayness and the darker humping of the hills.

Cold gripped the land at the tag end of the year, held it motionless, froze it into reluctant submission. West of town the hills were close. Stippled with pine and cedar except for a widening, raw-stumped, logged-out area, they brooded with icy regard over the flats. The wind came from behind them. It pushed an ominous haze toward the five riders drawing to a halt on the long ridge above Labelle.

Ira Flint settled wearily in the saddle of Ben Codine's big black stallion. He felt the sting of icy snow against his cheeks, whipped up from the crust which bound the land. He disliked the cold and he hated this land, but none of this showed in his face as he stared down at the town. He made a solid figure in sheepskin coat, a three-day beard pushed its blond stubble over his hard jaw and lean cheeks.

He worked his gloved hands to get some

warmth into them. His eyes were on some spot beyond town, among the lower hills which cinched the narrow waist of the flats.

Ira Flint had come home after ten years of absence. There was no anticipation in him, nor warmth. He looked down on the scene where he had been born with the remote and cruel curiosity of a timber wolf pausing by an old lair.

His companions waited behind him, hunched against the bitter wind. Finally Ira turned his horse off the ridge and rode down into a small ravine where a tiny stream glinted like hammered silver in the fading light of day.

The others turned to follow.

The Kansas Kid remained behind for a brooding moment. He was staring down upon the town, fast losing outline in the early winter dark, watching the lamps prick their pinpoints of light through the gloom.

The wind muttered through the trees at his back. He could not have heard the sound of sleigh bells if there had been any. Yet some trick of memory made them sound in his ears, reminding him by association of Christmastime at home. The memory reached back a long way in time, yet it brought a lump to his throat. The Kid was not yet twenty, but he had not been home in eight years. He had no home to go to. Home was a word and a memory, mostly bitter, except for this time of year.

He blew on his gloved hands in absent-minded gesture, fighting the small knot of loneliness in his stomach. Reaction twisted his thin lips back from crooked, yellowing teeth; he brought up his sleeve to wipe his nose as he turned his shivering mount off the ridge to join the others.

Down in the ravine Wally Mavis sat stiffly in saddle, hating to dismount. His old bones were not used to this cold. He tried wrapping himself in the mentally-induced warmth of the Mexican sun but his numbed lips cursed the bleak bite of the wind.

He watched Flint tie Nig to a low-hanging limb along the creek bottom and loosen the big black's cinches. The others were dismounting behind them. He forced himself out of saddle and tied his mare beside the stallion. His thoughts went back to the man they had left to die. A faint uneasiness worked in him every time he remembered.

The big stallion had given Ira trouble from the beginning. It had fought the outlaw every chance he had. Now it waited docilely enough beside Wally's mare in final acceptance of the inevitable.

Wally sighed. He and Ira had picked up companions since that day he had rescued the tawny-haired killer from Ben Codine: Monk Ulley, Travis Paine and the Kansas Kid. The last three jobs had welded them into a tight unit. The one ahead of them promised to be the most profitable of their short, checkered career.

Labelle, booming under the impact of a fabulous silver strike, was planning the greatest New Year's celebration in its history. Despite the cold, a grin twitched Wally's lips.

Labelle, he reflected wryly, would have cause to remember this New Year's Day!

Monk had a small fire going. He and the Kansas Kid squatted around it, warming their hands. Monk was a bull-necked, burly man with a full black beard and a bulbous nose and hamlike, hairy hands that could twist a horseshoe out of shape.

He seemed a placid, dull ox of a man, yet his eyes were small and quick and he had a way with women. In Santa Fe he had broken the neck of a man whose woman he wanted. He had left her two days later. . . .

Travis Paine alone remained mounted, just outside the fireglow. A lean, grave-faced man just past the sharp edge of youth, he was also a taciturn man whose graying temples gave him, when he dressed the part, a scholarly, dignified air. But Wally knew the mean streak in the man which cropped up during his black moods. Only Ira could handle Travis then.

Flint was digging in his coat pocket for a letter. His long shadow shifted as he stepped away from the fire to hand it to Paine.

He said: "He's staying at the Baker House. Room 27." Ira watched Travis pocket the letter. "The Kid is set to be in the Elite Lunchroom at two, tomorrow afternoon. Don't keep him waiting. He'll have a six-mile ride back!"

Travis nodded. He waited, indifferent to the cold, a man caught up in his own thoughts. Flint cursed him in silent exasperation.

"Don't keep him waiting!" he repeated sharply.

Travis nodded coldly. "I'll be there, Ira." He turned his horse and faded into the darkness.

The Kansas Kid moved restlessly around the fire. "Damn this cold," he complained. Wally glanced at him, but neither he nor Monk sneered at the Kid. No one sneered at the Kid. Not even Ira, although Ira alone could shade the Kid to the draw.

Monk spat into the fire and listened to the sizzle. He turned to Flint coming back into the small glow of the flames. "How long?" he grunted.

"We'll give him twenty minutes," Flint replied.

"Travis has it soft this time," the Kid commented, his teeth chattered. "A hotel room, a warm meal —"

"We'll all have it soft," Flint broke in. He was standing close to the fire now, shaking tobacco onto brown cigarette paper. "You'll get all the hot grub you can stand where we're going to hole out."

"The Dodd place," the Kid said, remembering. "You've been there before?"

A sudden crashing among the horses picketed downstream jerked the Kid around, his hand streaking to the gun under his coat. Flint dropped his sack of tobacco into the fire; he was moving around the Kid, drawing his gun. Monk and Wally moved abruptly away from the revealing flames.

Flint reached the picketed horses first. He saw a dark bulk go crashing through the brush and merge into the thick shadows. In the same moment he made a quick inventory of the horses shifting in mild alarm along the small creek.

Ben Codine's big black stallion was gone!

Ira cursed harshly as he ran along the creek. The Kid paced grimly just behind him.

Nig was going over the ridge. It was too dark to see, but Flint caught a glimpse of the big animal as it topped the crest, a dark silhouette against the winter sky. He fired twice, knowing even as he pulled trigger that it was a futile gesture.

He stopped and the Kid pulled up beside him. "Pulled himself free an' hightailed it," the Kid muttered. "Thought you had left a saddle on him, though."

"I did!" Flint growled. "Loosened the cinches; he must have slipped it free through the brush."

"Think we can run him down?"

Flint shook his head. "Not this side of hell!" he said bitterly. "That cayuse's been waiting for a chance to get away since I forked him!" He turned back toward the fire, slipped his Colt back into holster.

"I'll ride behind Wally," he growled. "We'll see about you picking up a good animal for me in town tomorrow."

Wally and Monk were waiting by the fire. "Goddam stallion broke away," Flint explained. "Put out that fire. We'll divide the gear on the pack animal among your cayuses. I've just decided I'll ride the bay as far as the Dodd place."

They found Ira's saddle just below the ridge. The sharp wind cut through the thin layer of warmth the fire had given them. From the high slopes a gray timber wolf howled his hungry protest into the cold night. They rode into the wind, four silent, dangerous men.

The JD ranchhouse literally had been built with its back to the wall. It stood at the head of a narrow valley which had its good and its bad points, depending upon a man's angle of vision. The small, protected valley six miles out of Labelle had good graze for a limited number of cows; the Flats ranchers laughed at it.

But it was all that Jesse Dodd wanted; it was all that he could handle.

The five riders came to it in the night with a sleet storm building behind them. Ten years had changed nothing, Ira thought as he dismounted. He turned and fumbled in his saddle bag for a bottle.

The others were bunched behind him as he flung open the door.

They intruded upon a comfortable scene. Five unshaven callous killers, they walked into a living room warmed by a blazing log fire in the big stone fireplace and fragrant with new cut pine, making a bouquet on the table.

Martha Dodd was in her chair by the fire, a mending basket in her lap. Jesse Dodd was coming into the room from the kitchen ell, carrying a jug of cider.

Wally Mavis, last man in, kicked the door shut behind him.

Jesse, a small, stringy man in his forties, watched Ira walk to the table, sweep the Christmas pine off and place the whiskey bottle in its place.

"Happy New Year, Uncle Jess!"

Jesse Dodd stared. It was all of ten years since this man, a gangling boy then, had stolen the best of his two saddle horses and taken the fifty-seven dollars he had tucked

37

away under his straw mattress and left the JD. Jesse had never expected to see his unwed sister's son again.

"Ira!" The name stuck in his throat.

Martha leaned forward in her chair, peering nearsightedly at this man they had tried to raise after his mother's death. The face was vaguely familiar to her with its sullen cruelty about the mouth, but the boy she had known had been blond.

Flint was peeling off his gloves. He unbuttoned his coat, threw it over a chair. He turned and waved an arm that took in the room.

"Make yourselves at home, boys," he invited. "Aunt Martha will have supper for us as soon as she can get to the kitchen."

Jesse came to the table. His boots crunched on shards of earthenware from the bowl which had held the pine boughs. He placed the cider jug down. His voice held a choked fear.

"What do you want here, Ira? Why did you come back?"

"I came to wish you a happy New Year," Ira sneered. "I brought my friends with me."

From one of the bedrooms a girl called out: "Mother, do we have visitors?"

Flint turned to the door. Jesse put out a hand to stop him, but Flint shrugged it off.

The girl pushing herself up to sitting position against the headboard was pale and thin.

Her chestnut brown hair was braided into pigtails which fell upon each shoulder. A high-necked blue flannel nightgown hung loosely, not accentuating the fact that she was a woman.

She stopped her struggle to sit up at Flint's appearance. There was fear in her brown eyes as she stared at him.

"Hello, Theresa," Flint greeted. His voice was false, threaded with mockery. "Remember me? Ira? I used to pull your pigtails."

She pulled the covers up around her and shrank back against the headboard.

Ira laughed. "What's wrong with you, Theresa?" His sneer warped his mouth. "Too much celebrating?"

Blood put color in Theresa Dodd's face . . . as her mother, coming up, pulled Flint around to her. "Leave her alone!" she cried. "Leave us all alone! You've never been anything but trouble."

He shoved her back into the living room. "You haven't started to see the kind of trouble I can bring you," he snarled. "Get into the kitchen and rustle up some grub. Me and the boys are hungry." Turning, harsh-mouthed: "You, Uncle Jess, take care of our horses!"

Martha stood stubbornly beside her husband.

Flint's amber eyes slitted; there was a naked cruelty to the twist of his lips. His hand lifted Codine's big Peacemaker out of holster.

Jesse said bitterly: "Do as he wants, Martha. He . . . he'd kill us all."

Flint laughed. "Do as he wants, Martha," he mocked. He looked contemptuously at Dodd. "You always had more sense, Jess, but Aunt Martha had more guts!"

"How long are you staying?" The question was a whisper of defeat from the small man.

"Long enough to see the New Year in properly, eh, boys?" Flint's voice held a hidden laughter.

Jesse's shoulders sagged. He put on his threadbare coat and stepped out into the driving sleet.

Travis Paine rode into Labelle with the wind in his face. He pulled his hat brim over his eyes and pulled his neckerchief up to protect the lower half of his face. He rode past the freight yard and up Lodestone Avenue, lifting his head only to search out the building line for the one he wanted.

A cloth sign stretched across the street over his head flapped in the wind. Travis could not read it, nor was he interested.

He spotted The Baker House up beyond the sign, a three-story, twin-galleried wooden building, and he turned his tired mount to the rail. He walked into the lobby and silently appraised and was in turn appraised by the half-dozen men clustered about the pot-bellied stove.

At the desk he asked for a room on the second floor and got it. He signed his name, leaving out the *i* in Paine. He was not known in this part of the country, but caution was inbred in him.

He mentioned his horse and the clerk said there was a stable around the corner; one of the hotel help would take care of it for him, if Travis wished.

The hotel had a bar and a dining room, and Travis stopped in both places before going up to his room. He remained here only long enough to shuck his greatcoat, wash, shave, brush his hair. Then he stepped out into the hallway lighted by a lamp placed at each end, and walked softly until he came to room 27. He knocked.

He heard a rustle of paper, then a surly voice said: "Come in."

Travis stepped inside and closed the door. He let his gray eyes move from the man in the upholstered chair in quick survey of what seemed to him a rather plushily furnished room and onto an adjoining bedroom.

His sober glance came back to the man in the chair. A handsome man despite a receding hairline, a weak chin and gold-framed reading spectacles which seemed to magnify his cold blue eyes.

Travis said: "Paul Shaney?"

The man nodded.

"I'm Travis Paine. Flint sent me."

Shaney leaned forward. The paper he had been reading fell from his lap. "I was expecting Ira —"

"He'll see you later," Travis cut in coldly. "I'm the contact man." He unbuttoned the top of his coat, brushed the lapel aside to show Shaney the glitter of a silver badge. "Marshal Travis Paine. You can vouch for me."

Shaney frowned. "I don't know. . . ." Abruptly: "What has Ira planned?"

Travis put his glance on the bottle of bourbon on the table. "It was a long cold ride into town," he said quietly. "I ain't thawed out yet."

Shaney got up and went to a small cabinet for another glass. He waved Travis to a chair and poured generously. His eyes had a cold, calculating glint as he lifted his glass.

"To a happier and profitable New Year . . . Marshal."

IV

Aline Buskin waved goodbye to her father standing in the doorway of the small shack by the side of the rails and climbed into the buggy. She pulled the robe up about her legs and knees and picked up the reins.

The howl of a wolf pack rode the cutting wind; it made the bay between the buggy's shaft nervous. He tossed his head, fighting the bit.

"Take Tommy with you next time." Her father cupped his hands around his mouth to hurl the words at her. He didn't like the thought of his daughter riding out here in this weather just to bring him a hot dinner; he didn't like the sound of that wolf pack.

Aline nodded. She waved again and slapped the bay lightly across the withers with the loose ends of her reins. The animal moved against his collar, turning in a tight circle, and headed in a brisk trot away from the lonely switchman's shack up by Silver Gap.

The "norther" had brushed across the Lodestones, peppering the country with two inches of dry ice particles that bounced like coarse sand over the frozen earth. It had blown itself out by morning.

But the wind had an icy edge; it brought color to Aline's cheeks; a sparkle to her eyes. She was twenty-two, a "gal getting on in years" in this country. A tall, slender, well-fashioned girl with soft brown hair, dreamy blue eyes. She taught school in Labelle, and at twenty-two she was still unmarried.

Perhaps her mother was right, she thought; she read too many books, dreamed too much. It made her too choosy. She wanted a man like those in the books she read — a tall, handsome, gentle man to come riding into her life.

The baying of the wolf pack seemed suddenly close; it broke through her reverie with chilling implication. The bay started to pick up his gait, mincing with evident fright. His breath plumed like twin frosty banners before him.

A shiver went through her and for the first time since she had left the railroad shack she felt panic stir in her. She fought it, sitting tense in the jolting seat, her eyes ranging over that frozen land made stark by winter, a chromatic scene of black and white and dismal gray lid of sky.

She had emerged through the ridge out on the way to town and a long swale lay ahead, bordered by scrub timber. At the top of the far rise, she knew, she would be in sight of town, and this cheered her.

She gave the bay his head, sharing his eagerness to get back home. The narrow iron tires skidded in the frozen ruts, bouncing her around on the spring seat. She had to haul back, suddenly afraid of overturning the light vehicle.

The bay fought the restraint. The wolf pack was nearer; it seemed to be veering toward them. The bay shook his head, fighting the bit; his eyes rolled wildly.

"Easy, boy," she said, fighting down her own panic. "Slowly does it. They won't bother us."

She saw the horse then, topping the rise on her right. She saw him out of the corner of her eyes and she turned, a thin gasp catching in her throat.

He was riderless, a big, beautiful black stallion, dragging his reins. He came over the rise less than a hundred yards away, pausing to survey her. Even at this distance she could see his muscles quiver with fatigue.

Impulse made her pull the bay to a trembling stop. Her first thought was that someone was in trouble. The big black stud might have spilled his rider, leaving him to the grim mercy of that wolf pack.

But she had heard no shots. If the black's rider had been merely thrown, surely he. . . .

She stood up, which was a mistake. The big stallion started down the slope and suddenly foundered in a drift. He was very tired. But he fought desperately to get out to solid footing.

And it was at this moment that the first gray shape appeared on the slope behind the black stallion. The timber wolf paused, tongue lolling, eyeing the sorrel. Another loomed up beside him, silent as a drifting shadow. Behind the pitch of slope rose a howl of naked, savage hunger.

The bay lunged forward. The motion caught Aline by surprise, jerked her off balance. She fell against a corner of the buggy seat and a sharp pain stabbed through her side, wringing a cry from her lips. She tried to grasp something to hold onto, but her mittened fingers slid off and she fell from the moving buggy.

She fell heavily and the impact knocked the wind from her. But a sharp and terrible fear roused her. She scrambled to her feet and started to run after the buggy. She took a dozen faltering steps before the grim futility of her action stopped her. She stood stricken, watching the runaway bay top the far rise to town and disappear.

The sharp presence of danger turned her around then, her eyes widening. The big black stallion had fought his way clear of the snow drift. He came toward her now, too spent to keep running from that silent horde on the far rise.

He came toward her, reins dragging, as if seeking her human companionship in this final hour.

★ ★ ★

Harvey Buskin, chipping ice from around the track switch, paused to eye the rider coming toward him from the Silver Gap trail. The cutting wind made Harvey's eyes water. His breath made its frosty vapor with each exhalation, gray-white like his hair.

Few riders took this trail to Labelle at this time of the year. It was a whole lot more comfortable riding in one of the SP coaches.

But the man on the roan mare didn't look like the kind who thought a hell of a lot of his own comfort. He was a big man, even without the sheepskin coat covering his wide shoulders. His face, what Harvey could see of it above his coat collar and under his hat brim, was travel-gaunted, dark with beard stubble. But the eyes which surveyed him had a dark level glint; they had the remote curiosity of a cougar which had just fed.

The man clasped his hands on his saddle horn and leaned slightly forward. His voice was strangely gentle. "Lonely job."

Harvey rubbed his hands together to bring warmth into them. "Been my job for ten years." He was suspicious of strangers, all strangers who looked like this man, hard, gunned, and with no good reason to be out riding in weather like this. His suspicions ground into his voice, bringing a thin gleam to the rider's eyes.

"Labelle . . . ?" He made the one word a

question; he obviously was not a garrulous man.

Harvey turned and pointed toward the ridge cut. "Follow the rails."

The cry of the wolf pack came on the wind; it made Ben's mare lift her head and cock her ears back.

Harvey frowned. "Looks like a bad winter," he said, as if to explain the wolf pack. "Don't usually hear them so close to town."

He was thinking of Aline who had left not too long ago. He stifled the anxiety that pinched his mouth. It wasn't likely they'd attack a woman driving this close to Labelle.

Ben Codine's glance followed the older man's; he saw the narrow buggy tracks on the hard snow and some inkling of the man's anxiety came through to him. His gaze moved past these to the rails knifing through the ridge ahead. He didn't say anything, but he was a man who missed little.

He put his glance on Harvey again. His voice had a flatness now, as though the words he spoke had been asked many times.

"See a man about my size ride this way? Forking a big black stud?"

Harvey shook his head. "You're the first stranger I've talked to since the cold set in. Better'n two weeks ago." He caught the faint glint of disappointment in those cold, level eyes and something obscure in him made him add: "There are other trails into Labelle."

"So there are," Codine murmured. He nodded slightly. "Don't let those wolves get too close, Pop," he grinned, and moved on.

Harvey let his eyes follow the tall rider into the ridge cut. The wind blew steadily, cold and sharp and making its senseless mutter overhead. But it was more than the wind which sent a shiver through him.

The baying of the wolf pack sounded again, a chilling sound flung against the gray winter sky. The roan mare under the bounty hunter trembled; she snorted softly, not liking the nearness of that savage pack.

Ben put his narrowing gaze to the trail ahead, appraising the narrow treads of the buggy. Whoever was driving could not be too far ahead, and it occurred to him then that the man might be in trouble.

He touched heels to the mare and sent her lunging ahead; he was breaking out of the ridge cut when he heard Aline scream!

The bounty hunter jerked his rifle free from scabbard and levered a shell home; then he broke out of the hemmed-in trail and the scene opened up to him.

Surprise shocked through his lean frame, making his pull-back on his reins harshly cruel. The mare squatted, slid to a trembling stop; one word broke from Ben Codine's tight lips:

"Nig!"

The big stallion stood across the road ahead,

less than a hundred yards from Ben, a wild and magnificent animal, rearing up, forefeet held ready to lash out at the snarling gray shapes ringing him.

Close to him, her left shoulder almost brushing that satiny black hide, a terrified girl stood with her hand to her mouth. She didn't see Ben. Her eyes were on the big brindle timber wolf edging toward her. She saw him settle back to jump, and the scream that tore from her lips seemed to merge into Ben's sharp rifle crack!

The wolf was beginning his spring when the slug hit him. Reflex kicked him upward in an aimless, grotesque leap. He fell limply at Aline's feet and Nig whirled and came down on that quivering carcass with iron-shod hoofs.

Ben's rifle scattered the others like gray leaves hit by a powerful gust of wind. They were gone before the last rifle crack faded against the cold sky, leaving three of their number still bulks against the snow and a fourth, hind legs useless, dragging himself toward the brush.

Ben Codine's last shot finished him.

The black stallion was standing over the mangled carcass, ears still flattened wickedly. He turned to face the rider coming toward him; bit irons made their steely sound as he tossed his head in sudden recognition. A tired whicker of gladness came from him.

Ben rode up to the big, spent stallion. He ran his hand along that tired neck, his voice thick with emotion. "Nig, boy. . . ."

It was all of three months since he had lost this big stallion; there had been times on the trail when he had felt lost without him. From the day the bounty hunter had put his saddle on this powerful stallion, they had been inseparable.

Nig turned to muzzle his shoulder, and then Ben noticed the girl, white-faced, staring, her eyes dark now with a growing wonder.

Forgetting her presence, Ben had put a seldom-glimpsed side of him on display for her, a sentimental streak usually buried deep inside him. He felt the beginning of a flush warm his cheeks, then an iron discipline took control; his hand lifted to touch his hat brim in acknowledgment of her presence.

"Sorry, ma'am. I didn't mean to overlook —"

He caught the quick fluttering of her eyelids and the deepening pallor of her face; he was mentally berating himself for being an unfeeling fool as he slid quickly out of saddle.

He caught her before she fell.

She lay limply in his arms, her face pressed against his shoulder. He thought she had fainted. Then a shudder went through her, and she began to cry, the broken, half-stifled crying of relief.

Ben held her, seemingly weightless, in his arms. He felt her softness, and her crying stirred him; it had been a long time since he had heard a woman cry. It pulled at him with vague tentacles that had their roots in the past, and pointed up his essential loneliness.

Her face turned away from his coat and up to him. Color fought its way back into her pale face; the wet brightness of her eyes mirrored self shame.

"Put me down, please." Her voice was low, held back, as if she did not quite trust it. "I'm all right . . . now."

Ben smiled at her. It broke the harsh planes of his face, that smile; it made him look younger, almost boyish, despite the dark stubble on his face. It was a smile that reached deep behind those level gray eyes.

"I'm glad to hear that," he replied. "I'm afraid I behaved rather rudely, ma'am —"

"It isn't ma'am," she cut in on him, a tremulous smile on her lips. "And you can put me down now?"

Ben set her down on her feet. Nig nudged him, wanting attention, and Aline Buskin, feeling strangely breathless and warm now, was glad to have him turn those smiling eyes from her.

"Why, this beautiful horse seems to know you!" she exclaimed.

Ben nodded. "He should. I . . . lost him about three months ago."

"Oh!" She shivered now as the cold wind reached through her coat. "Have you been looking for him all this time?"

"And for the man who stole him," Ben said. His voice had gone bleak as the gray day. "I thought I was following someone in a buggy. I didn't expect to find you, or Nig." He let his statement hang suspended between them, waiting for her to fill in.

"I *was* driving a buggy," Aline said quickly. She told him what had happened. "I thought at first his rider had been thrown. But now I don't know."

Ben turned his glance to the trail the big stallion had made coming down the slope. It was possible Nig had managed to throw Flint, but he doubted it had happened recently. Nig looked as though he had been running for a long time.

The girl's voice brought his attention back to her. "I'm Aline Buskin," she said. "You probably saw my father, if you came by way of the Gap road?"

Ben nodded. "I'm . . . Ben," he said. He was abruptly aware that the name Codine had been making headlines these past weeks; it was not a good name to use just now.

A faint shadow brushed across Aline's eyes, but her smile seemed to brighten. "Ben. It's a nice name." She held out a mittened hand to him, but the movement brought a sharp pain knifing through her side. She winced.

"I forgot I bruised myself against the side of the seat," she whispered.

The bounty hunter picked her up again. "I'll get you home. Before someone spots that buggy of yours going into town without a driver and comes out with blood in his eye."

He lifted her astride the roan's saddle, turned to gather up Nig's reins. The big stallion was in no condition to be ridden today. He mounted behind Aline, sliding his right arm around her trim waist.

It was not the way Ben Codine had expected to enter Labelle, but he had no regrets.

V

They came into town along the railbed, swinging away from the rails to cross the narrow, steep-banked creek over a small plank bridge.

Labelle still retained the raw look of a town newly born — ramshackle structures with unpainted false fronts, green boards which had warped and weathered badly. But it was a deceiving layer, like the skin of an orange. The center of Labelle was solid. Two-and-three-story structures lined Lodestone Avenue, several of them of gray stone blocks.

There was money in Labelle, and it was reflected in the variety of its shops, in the neatly lettered windows testifying to the presence of an attorney-at-law, mining stock brokers, a dentist — even a piano teacher offering lessons at $2.00 per hour.

Aline Buskin had talked about herself on the way to town. She had told Ben of her father and mother and Tommy, her younger brother, and little of her job as schoolteacher. She had talked of herself because Ben seemed inclined to say nothing, and the silences she had allowed to fall between them only made her conscious of the strong arm about her waist and the physical nearness of this big man who had come riding into her life.

She was still talking as Ben turned up Lodestone Avenue and pulled the roan mare in quickly toward the near walk as a buggy bore down on them.

The man in the seat was small and shapeless in his heavy coat. He saw Ben and the girl riding in front of Codine as he swept by and he brought the bay up in a squatting slide. His black, piercing eyes held a bright relief as he tooled the buggy around and toward Codine and the girl.

His grayshot, drooping mustache waggled with his grin. "Shore glad to see you, Aline. Had a downright bad moment when I saw Rebel come into the yard draggin' rein an' nobuddy in the seat."

His gaze shifted from the girl to the bounty hunter, and he made note of the big black stallion trailing close behind. A small, questioning frown dimmed the light in his eyes.

"It was very kind of you to come looking for me, Rio," Aline said. She turned to Ben. "This is Rio Vegas, Ben. He owns the livery stable closest to the Baker House."

Ben nodded slightly. "Miss Buskin had an accident, Rio. I happened to be on the road behind her when the bay bolted and left her afoot."

"Left me facing a pack of hungry wolves," she broke in, shuddering. She told Vegas what had happened to her, making it short but clear.

"Figgered Rebel had run into a pretty bad scare, the way he showed up," the stableman nodded. He let his glance take in the big stallion again, but his voice was puzzled. "You say that big stud was runnin' loose?"

"Not any more," Ben put in coldly. "I'm claiming him."

There was a coldness in the bounty hunter's tone that discouraged probing. Vegas shrugged. He turned to Aline. "I'll drive you home, if you wish."

"I'll see Miss Buskin home," Ben said. "But I'll be obliged to you if you'd take the stud in. He needs to be rubbed down, grained and rested. I'll drop by to settle the bill."

The livery man nodded. "Glad to," he said gruffly. He stepped down from the buggy and took the black stallion's reins from Ben. He looped them around the whip socket, and turned to the tired animal.

Nig pulled back at his reins, turning to whicker questioningly to the bounty hunter. Codine reached over to rub the big stallion's ear. "I'll see you, Nig. Go with him."

Rio's black eyes crinkled thoughtfully. "Seems to have taken to you already, Ben."

"Not already," Codine said levelly. "We're really old friends." He watched Nig trot alongside the buggy as Rio drove away. The stallion kept looking back, until they reached the corner.

Aline murmured: "Three blocks ahead, Ben. Then turn right."

The Buskins lived off Lodestone, in the quiet section of town. A small frame house, painted white but beginning to show the ravages of a hard winter, it was enclosed by a low picket fence and faced with a wide front porch running the width of the house.

Ben helped Aline down and pushed open the gate and walked with her to the front door. It opened as they stepped up to the porch where a stout woman, shorter than Aline but with a family resemblance of features, met them. She looked at Ben with frowning reserve.

Aline said: "It's all right, mother, I wasn't kidnapped." Her laughter was light, but she saw her mother look keenly at her, as though she sensed something behind Aline's voice. The lightness dropped from it, became serious. "I . . . I had a terrible fright on the way back from bringing Pa's dinner. If it hadn't been for Ben . . ." She turned to the bounty hunter, and Codine knew she was expecting him to add more to the name. He kept silent.

A lanky boy of fourteen loomed up in the hallway behind the woman. He listened to his sister's story.

"Come in, come in!" Mrs. Buskin exclaimed then. "Land's sake, it's no way to thank you, keeping you waiting out in the cold."

Ben smiled. "It's thanks enough to have been of help, Mrs. Buskin. But I must go. I have some business to attend to."

"Well, in that case. . . ." The older woman looked to her daughter, catching the shadow of disappointment in Aline's eyes. She smiled warmly. "You'll come tonight, then? For supper? I don't think you'll regret it, young man." Her eyes twinkled. "I do make the best chicken dumplings in town, and I can prove it."

Ben's smile widened. "In that case, how can I refuse?" He touched fingers to his hat.

"Goodbye, Aline."

The girl stood in the doorway, watching the tall figure move down the walk to the waiting roan. Her brother squeezed in beside her, a teasing grin on his freckled face.

"And Lochinvar came riding out of the West," he quoted, and jumped back as his sister whirled on him. His mother said severely: "Now, Tommy, stop that!"

"It's in the book she's reading to us in school," Tommy said. "Me an' Bighead like that part best. About young Lochinvar. . . ."

"Bighead and I," Aline corrected, flushing.

"Yeah, Bighead and I," Tommy repeated, grinning impudently.

The two men coming out of the Baker House stopped as Ben Codine rode by the hotel.

Paul Shaney muttered: "That's him, Travis. He had the Buskin girl with him a few minutes ago, and a big black stallion trailing behind."

Travis Paine let his glance take in the bounty hunter. He felt moody today, his nerves were taut. He needed a drink, a lot of drinks. But he knew when this gray mood came over him the drinks were no solution.

"Where's the big stud now?" he asked curtly.

"Rio Vegas took him with him . . . back to the stable, I guess." Shaney's eyes followed the rider. "Looks like he's headed that way now."

Paine frowned. If the stallion Shaney was talking about was the one Ira had been riding, it was possible the stranger had run across him and brought him in. Any man would jump at the chance to claim that big stallion. But something about the rider who had just passed troubled Paine; he looked a lot like Ira, from a distance.

He said shortly: "I'll keep an eye on him, Paul."

Ben Codine rode past these two men on the hotel veranda; he saw them, noted their frowning interest, and his mind filed them away for future reference. The cloth sign ahead of him flapped sharply in the wind, drawing his attention. He read the cheerful welcome:

60

A HAPPY NEW YEAR TO ALL . . .
JAKE GRADY

Ben saw this and it reminded him of other years; he saw them slip by in his thoughts, full and turbulent years. Old friends, places, the width and breadth of Texas were in those years. Men he had known, now dead — men like Sawtelle Smith, Whispering Collins, the Tenafly brothers.

For Ben Codine the tag end of the year had always been a lonely time. Since the time he had buried his wife and child, the year-end holidays had been a bad period for him. Now he felt the warmth creep along his right arm where Aline's slender figure had nestled. She was a woman a man could get used to. He shoved the unfinished thought aside. He had decided long ago that he could never ask any woman to share his kind of life.

So Ben put his thoughts to the man he had searched a score of towns for, sifting each fragment of conversation, weighing each answer to his questions.

Flint's trail had led north and then west. Sometimes it had faded altogether, and he had swung wide before picking up a thread of the man's movements again.

But it was blind luck, he knew, running across the black stallion here. Labelle had been just another town to come to and ask his grim questions. He had not expected to find Flint here.

But finding the black stud pinned Flint down. The outlaw was here somewhere. In town. Or hiding out close by. Somewhere in the vicinity Flint was waiting. And knowing the pattern, if not the details, of the man's thinking, Ben knew that Flint had come to Labelle for only one reason: a holdup.

The bounty hunter was finally closing in on his quarry, but from here on it was going to be ticklish game. For the first time in his career Ben Codine was riding outside the law.

A half-dozen counties had dodgers out for him, although no picture of Ben Codine graced them. His brother-in-law, Sheriff Tolliver, had made every effort to suppress this, and had succeeded in most.

But here in Labelle Ben was on his own. In a pinch he would produce Sheriff Tolliver's letter, but at best it would mean little more than a delay. The delay would give his quarry time to get away.

He was at the corner where Rio Vegas had turned with the buggy, and the building at his elbow, as he made the turn, bore the over-the-door sign: DUTCH'S TAVERN. He rode past it, finding another sign facing him; a painted black arm with pointing finger: VEGAS LIVERY STABLES.

The big two-decker barn lay back from the road. Ben rode between wheel tracks rutting the frozen ground, and the mare's hoofs clumped on the wooden ramp leading to the barn door.

Vegas appeared in the narrow opening, glanced at Ben, and put his shoulder to the big door, pushing it back on its iron runners. The sharply pungent, warm smell of horses and manure washed out to the bounty hunter.

He rode the mare inside, behind Vegas, and dismounted. Nig was in one of the stalls; he lifted his head over the boards and whistled to Ben.

Vegas had a curry comb in his hand as he came up to Ben. "If that stud was mine, I'd be combing the country for him," he said.

"I've been looking for him for six weeks," Ben replied drily.

Vegas frowned. "I thought you said you found him running loose up by the Southern Pacific ridge cut?"

"I did," Ben nodded. "I'm interested in the man who rode him here. A man about my size, my build; could pass for my brother. You see him?"

The stableman shook his head. "Yores is the first strange face I've seen in two weeks. Nope, wait a minnit. Stranger rode in just last night. I didn't see him. One of the hotel help brought his horse over. He's stayin' at the Baker House."

He walked along the stalls and motioned to a rangy gray. "That's his cayuse."

Ben looked the animal over. The brand, a lopsided star, was not one he recognized.

"Baker House, you say?" He was thinking of the two men on the hotel veranda who had looked him over as he rode by.

Vegas nodded. "Just up the street. You must have ridden by it, comin' here."

He watched Ben leave. And after Ben had gone the picture of the big, quiet man remained in his thoughts, nagging at him. Before he had settled in Labelle Rio Vegas had been remuda boss with the OBL, one of the big trail outfits. He had seen some dangerous gunslingers in the trail towns; they walked like this man who had just left: easy, yet coiled like a steel spring.

Vegas sucked in a deep breath. Labelle had been quiet too long. The usual brawls among the miners, an occasional shooting over a woman. But nothing that deputy sheriff Mido Peters couldn't handle.

But Rio Vegas had the uneasy feeling that this year would not end peacefully. He tried to shrug the feeling off as he turned back to work on the big stallion, but the sense of violence in the air persisted, nagging at him.

VI

Dutch's Tavern had a few card tables, a long, plain bar and a well-stocked liquor cellar. Some of it was on display on back shelves. Otherwise no fancy trimmings. No percentage girls. It was strictly a drinking establishment. At the end of the bar, where it made a short right angle to the wall, was a free lunch counter stocked with liverwurst, thick slices of home-made dark bread, pickles, boiled eggs.

Ben found a place at the bar and ordered whiskey and listened to the swirl of conversation around him. A lot of it had to do with Jake Grady and the big celebration the owner of the Shamrock mine was giving New Year's Eve.

"Money ain't changed old Jake one bit," one man laughed. "Spent over a quarter of a million dollars on that sheebang of his on the hill. Twenty rooms and a half-dozen bath tubs like they got in them fancy Eastern hotels. Built it for his wife, he says, but Jake spends most of his time in town playing poker with his old friends."

Codine let the talk soak in. The second whiskey began to warm him. He caught the busy bartender's eye and ordered a refill.

The man lingered long enough to observe cheerfully: "Stranger in town?"

Ben nodded. He was turned sidewise to the counter, and he saw the two men who came in; he had passed them not too long ago, standing on the steps of the Baker House.

"I got a cussed poor memory," Ben murmured, "but it seems to me I should know those two gents who just came in. Maybe you can help jog the recollection some. Who are they?"

The bartender squinted through the smoke haze. "Man with the glasses is Paul Shaney, Grady's bookkeeper," he replied. "Never laid eyes on the other man before." He turned away as someone at the far end of the bar yelled for service.

Shaney and Travis came to the bar, wedging into the space beside Ben. Shaney appeared nervous. He called to the bartender and asked for a special brand of whiskey; his hand shook as he poured, pushing a glass to Travis.

Travis was at the bounty hunter's shoulder and Codine looked him over. An inch or so shy of Ben's height, he was a quiet-appearing man. A flat-crowned black hat sat squarely on his head. But the tip of his holster, showing below his coat, was thonged down; and to Ben, whose job had been trailing dangerous men, this was a warning.

A moody man and a dangerous one, he

66

judged. Then put his gaze briefly on Shaney, measuring and dismissing this man in that one glance.

A small man with a petulant arrogance dimmed now by some troubling anxiety — that was how Ben pegged Paul Shaney.

Travis tossed his drink down. He made no face, nor did the shock of that raw whiskey show in his eyes. Only after the sixth or seventh drink would there be any indication that he had been drinking, and then only as a cruel dark fire building in his gaze.

He filled his glass again and turning, slid the bottle to Ben in open invitation. His tone held only a casual interest.

"Stranger in town, feller?"

"Just rode in," Ben admitted. He took the invitation and refilled his glass.

"Visiting friends?"

Ben shook his head.

Travis Paine gulped his drink. The empty glass made a sharp sound as he set it down on the bar. "Might be you're on business?"

Ben's eyes met the other's narrowing gaze and a bleakness came to his face. "It's mine," he said shortly.

Paine's mouth pinched at the corners. He lifted a hand to his coat lapel and pulled it aside. A brief gesture, held just long enough for Codine to catch the glitter of a deputy U.S. Marshal's badge!

"My business, too," Paine said. His voice was low, flat, stony.

Ben shrugged. The last thing he wanted right now was to get entangled with a federal officer.

He said, straight-faced: "Came to Labelle to meet a man. I'm a horse trader." He finished his drink, murmured, "Thanks, Marshal," and stepped away from the bar before Travis could think of anything to say.

The Kansas Kid came to town to keep his appointment with Paine; he did not know it was to be an appointment with death!

He rode in with his habitual sneer pasted to his narrow face, an open defiance to the world at large, a so-what attitude inbred and unshakeable. He had been beaten and shunted around as a child, a snot-nosed kid too small of body to earn respect, until he discovered a natural affinity with a six-gun and dedicated himself to its use. From the time he had killed his first man, no one had pushed him around or talked to him with disrespect and lived.

He came to Labelle just past the noon hour, a small figure hunched in his coat. He spied the Elite Lunchroom where he was to meet Travis, but he had more than an hour to kill and the one soft spot in the Kid was the spotted mare he rode. He took better care of that animal than he did of himself.

He reined in to the walk and questioned the first passerby who waved directions to the Vegas stables.

Ben Codine stepped out of Dutch's Tavern in time to watch the Kansas Kid ride past. His eyes followed that small figure, retaining a mental image of a narrow, pinched face, a tight sneer; and then the tumbler of recognition clicked into place.

Ben was alert now, a grim anticipation tingling through him. No strangers in Labelle in two weeks. And then a U.S. Marshal arrived, and now the Kansas Kid. The Marshal's appearance could be coincidence, but the bounty hunter had a sudden hunch that the Kid had not come to Labelle alone.

He turned and followed the Kid to the stables.

Rio Vegas had just finished with Nig when the Kid came to the door. He let him in and watched the newcomer dismount, snarl a curse at the weather and turn to him as if expecting an argument. The Kid was cold, and when he was cold he was edgy.

He found no argument in Rio. He loosened his coat, letting the rank warmth of the stable seep through to his wiry body. Vegas could see the two guns strapped to the Kid's thighs.

A youngster with only the beginnings of a beard, standing no taller than the stableman, yet a chill went through Rio. Labelle was suddenly receiving an influx of strangers, and the premonition of trouble rode hard through Vegas' uneasy speculations.

The Kid gave orders concerning the care and feeding of his mare and tacked a blunt question to the end of them. "What bar you recommend, Pop?"

"Dutch's place, just around the corner," Vegas answered. "Serves the best whiskey in town."

The Kid started to turn away. He caught the movement of the big black stallion several stalls down and he tensed. He stepped back against the wall, a catlike softness in the way he placed his booted feet down. His voice whipped at the stableman.

"That black stud, Pop? How'd it get here?"

Vegas felt the danger in the boy's voice; his own voice thickened: "Stranger brought him in about an hour ago."

The Kid slid along the wall until he came to Nig's stall. The stallion bared his teeth, recognizing the Kid, and the youngster's eyes narrowed. It was the big stud which had broken away from them last night; he'd know that powerful stallion anywhere.

He whirled on Vegas. "You know the man who brung him in? Know where he's staying?"

Vegas licked his lips. "The Baker House I think he said."

"Right here, Kid!" the bounty hunter filled in coldly. He blocked the barn door opening, a big man with an easy stride. He moved inside and away from the opening as the Kid turned his attention to him, the sneer riding high on the Kid's lips.

A big man with a gun riding hard against his right thigh, but neither the gun nor Ben's bigness impressed the Kid. A dead ringer for Ira, he thought, and then the grim implication of this hit him like a fist in his stomach.

Ben Codine — the bounty hunter!

It didn't square with the story Ira Flint had told them. Codine was dead! And yet. . . .

"I brought the black stud in," Ben was saying. "Found him out on the Flats." The bounty hunter's tone held a steel edge. "You claiming him?"

The Kid shook his head. "My mistake, mister. He looks a lot like the stud a friend of mine —" He bit his lips, realizing too late he had said too much.

Ben paused a few feet from him. "Could be you're right," he baited. "Where is your friend?"

The Kid shrugged. It had been a long time since he had been afraid of any man and it was not fear that made him turn away from Ben Codine, but caution. He shook his head, the sneer burning bright in his eyes. He walked past Ben, toward the door. But with

71

each step the thin leash rope of his caution pulled taut, began to unravel.

Codine faced around, knowing he had to stop the Kid from leaving. The outlaw was his link to Ira Flint; allowing him to get away would be to warn Flint he was in Labelle, on his heels.

His voice rang sharply along the stalls. "Kid! It's a long way back to Kansas! You'll never make it running."

The Kid was almost at the opening. He kept walking, as though he had not heard Ben's taunt. When he moved, it was without warning. He pivoted and drew in one pantherish motion and the gun in his hand was barely levelling when the bounty hunter's bullet found him.

The shots filled the barn with sound and the frightened animals lunged against their stall boards. Gunsmoke made a gray-blue haze in the passageway, its acrid bite making the horses snort.

Ben came through it to stand over the Kid's huddled figure. Vegas moved out of the empty stall where he had sought refuge; he stood to one side, looking down impassively at the body.

Ben felt the settling weight of disappointment in him. He had not wanted to kill the Kid, but the Kansas killer had been too fast, and Ben had not had time to place his shots.

Only one aspect of this ugly business gave

him a thin satisfaction: he was sure now that Ira Flint was in Labelle.

Men began looming up, blotting out the daylight streaming through the doorway. Travis was among them. The U.S. Marshal pushed his way to the Kid and glanced down at the body and Ben spotted the faint tremor in the man's shoulders. But if the lawman had recognized the Kid, he said nothing.

There was movement in the crowd behind Travis. A rangy man with a hard-planed face dominated by a stiff red brush of a mustache pushed through to the Marshal's side. He glanced at Travis, frowned, slid his cold blue eyes over the crumpled body at his feet and put his hard gaze on Ben. But his voice was directed at Vegas.

"What happened in here, Rio?"

Vegas glanced nervously at Ben. "He and the —" he indicated the Kid's body — "they had an argument over a horse. That big black stud over there."

Mido Peters, deputy sheriff, said grimly, "I want to know exactly what happened, Rio. You were here. Who started the argument?"

Vegas told him. "The kid was leaving and he, Ben, said, 'It's a long way back to Kansas' and that was when the kid started shooting."

"Ben?" Peters cut in on Vegas. "You know this man?"

Vegas looked at Codine; he moved his shoulders. "He was in here earlier, this morning."

Peters moved away toward Nig's stall. It added up to a shootout between two strangers over a horse. He wasn't particularly concerned about it; he knew neither of the two men. But strangers riding into Labelle always bothered him. He turned to Ben, his voice biting through the murmurings from the crowd.

"What about this horse? Whose is it?"

"Mine," Ben said coldly. "The Kid seemed to think it belonged to a friend of his."

Peters shook his head. "Damn funny mistake to make." He moved closer to the stall. "Can you prove he's yours?"

"I don't carry a bill of sale with me," Ben answered. "But I think I can prove it to you." He walked up to Nig and the stallion muzzled him affectionately. Ben said softly: "Freeze." The big stallion obeyed, became a black statue. "Okay," Ben said, stroking the arched neck. He pointed to the Kid's body. "Know him, Nig?"

The stallion turned his head; his teeth bared wickedly.

Peters grunted. "If he ain't your cayuse you sure made friends in a hurry," he acknowledged. But his eyes remained hard and suspicious and his voice was truculent.

"Vegas called you Ben," he growled. "Ben what?"

Codine hesitated. He measured this man in that moment, judging the streak of obstinacy in Peters, gauging the temper of the man. His kind could be prodded into stiff-backed anger that left dangerous speculation behind.

"Could be Smith," he said, and his voice held the faint touch of contempt in it.

He saw the dark surge of anger in Peters and he knew he had guessed correctly; the deputy's jaw angled sharply toward him. "All right, Smith! What are you doing in Labelle?" He caught Ben's glance toward the Kid and he rephrased the question, his anger riding him hard. "Why are you here?"

"I followed a road," Ben said bleakly.

Peters' hand dropped to his gun butt, his voice came thick in his throat. "All right, Smith! There's a road leading into town and one leading out! I'll give you until tomorrow morning to take the one leading out!"

He turned on his heel and ground his anger into the tone of his voice as he directed the men crowding around the Kid's body. "Two or three of you get him out of here, over to Saul's Funeral Parlor. The rest of you break it up."

He looked back to Ben.

"Until tomorrow morning!" he repeated grimly, and stamped out.

VII

Mido Peters stood at the window of his office and looked out into the busy street. A break in the leaden sky lay a splash of wan sunlight across the rutted road and he stared at it without seeing it, his thoughts sour and displeasing.

His two special deputies, hired for the holiday season, were out patrolling the town now with orders to be lenient with all but the worst offenders. Peters had three cells in the block behind him and he saw no point in crowding them with drunken, but otherwise harmless, miners.

He had other worries nagging at him, the more irritating because they were formless. The shooting in Vegas' stable bothered him, not so much for what happened as some disturbing premonition it seemed to stir in him.

Two strangers in a shootout over a horse. It could mean nothing more than that. And yet. . . .

He took a cigar from his vest pocket and bit off the end, his gray eyes moody. The end of another year. He had watched them come and go in Labelle . . . eight of them. He had arrived here when the Lucky Try gold mine was booming and remained after it had petered out. He had turned his hand from hardrock miner to town marshal, and a year later he had been voted deputy sheriff also, to give him wider jurisdiction.

He was thirty-one but he looked older. His face had a stiff, granite cast, seamed with harsh, unbending lines. His gray eyes looked at a man with cold, direct appraisal. Peters had seen enough of human nature not to trust it; he was curious only to the point where it concerned him. He was honest.

His thoughts drifted around the core of his uneasiness, to the celebration Jake Grady would be giving tomorrow night in the big ballroom of his monstrosity of a house.

Jake Grady was Labelle; he was the legend and the proof of its phenomenal growth. Jake had come to the Lodestones late; he had poked around the hills after the gold had petered out and most of Labelle's shrinking population had believed the town dead. He was looking for gold, too, but his Irish luck and an honest assayer had combined to produce the Shamrock, a hill deep-veined with almost pure silver.

Money had not made any discernible changes in Jake. He had splurged only once, when he built that twenty-room house on the small hill east of town. With Irish blarney, grown somewhat thin over the disappointing years, he had promised his wife that he would one day build her a castle to rival those in Killarney, and he kept his word.

But neither Jake nor his wife lived in it. For the greater part of the year they left it to the servants Jake had hired; they preferred to live in the Baker House, occupying the downstairs suite, close to the people they knew.

This year, like the others since he had become rich, Labelle was Jake's town. Starting at noon the last day of the year, the drinks in every bar in town would be on the house, the bill footed by Grady.

But this New Year's Day Jake had planned a surprise for the men who worked for him. A surprise only Mido Peters and Harmon Andrews, the banker, were let in on, besides Jake.

The surprise was a thousand-dollar bill. One to each man who worked for the Shamrock, from superintendent to swamper. One hundred and fifty-five men . . . one hundred and fifty-five thousand dollars!

The money meant nothing to Jake Grady. But it was a headache for Peters. New Year's Day would find half of Labelle drunk and the other half well on its way. One hundred and fifty-five thousand dollars would be floating around in a leather satchel, from the depot to the Shamrock office, and it would be his responsibility to see that nothing happened to it or to Jake Grady.

Little wonder that Mido Peters was suspicious of every stranger who came to town.

He became aware of the cigar in his mouth, unlighted, and he reached in his pocket for a wood match. The two men loomed up by the window and paused by the door and Mido held his hand, wondering what Paul Shaney wanted of him.

"Come in," he growled at the knock.

Grady's bookkeeper stepped inside first. The man behind him closed the door; he turned and put his glance in a swift appraisal of the law office before he relaxed.

Mido faced around, scowling. Another stranger. He had seen this man among the group around the Kid's body, but the man had disappeared before he had thought to question him.

The newcomer came bluntly to the point of his visit. "I'm Travis Paine," he said quickly. "United States Marshal." He showed Mido his badge, took out an identification card, held it out to the lawman.

Peters took it, a puzzled light in his eyes. He glanced at the card and saw that it verified Travis Paine's status, but Mido had never seen a deputy U.S. Marshal before and he did not know what sort of identification they carried.

Shaney said: "I can vouch for Travis, Peters. It was I who wrote to the Territorial office for him."

Peters scowled. "Grady's orders?"

Shaney shook his head. "You know how

Jake is," he said. "He leaves the worrying to others, like you and me." Shaney carried it off well enough, with a faint trace of bitterness in his tone; he knew Mido Peters had not been told of his juggling of the Shamrock books.

Mido nodded. He had forgotten that Paul Shaney was in a position to know about the money coming in by special train on New Year's Day.

Travis said smoothly: "I was headed this way anyway, Sheriff. I received a tip that that bounty hunter, Ben Codine . . . the one who turned outlaw . . . was on his way to the Lodestones and I —"

"*Codine!*" Peters stiffened, the formless, nagging worry in him taking shape now.

"That big fellow in Rio Vegas' barn, the gunman who called himself Smith . . ."

Travis interrupted easily: "Could be the man I'm after. He fits that bounty hunter's general description well enough."

Peters considered this. If the man was Ben Codine, he was going to be dangerous to handle. He eyed Travis narrowly. "Just what do you expect me to do about him, Marshal?"

Shaney answered nervously, before Travis could speak. "Jail him, Peters! Kill him if he resists arrest!"

The deputy sheriff's eyes went dark with unrestrained contempt. Travis saw this and edged in smoothly: "Maybe that isn't the best way, Peters. We're not sure that he is that renegade bounty hunter. But it does add up to the tip I got, and Codine is known to ride a big black stallion."

Peters nodded, his thoughts crowding a heavy V over his eyes. "That's what's bothering me, Marshal. If that big fellow is Codine, what's he stirred up trouble for already? Who's the man he gunned down in Vegas' barn? I had a talk with the livery man afterward, and he says this hombre claimed he'd found the big stud running loose outside of town."

"It might be a trick!" Shaney snapped, unwilling to relinquish his position. "What does it matter about the horse, or the man he killed? If he is Ben Codine there's going to be trouble. Best thing you can do right now is to jail him before it starts, Peters!"

The deputy sheriff's dark gaze turned on the bookkeeper. "You want to come with me when I take him?"

Shaney backed away. "Hell, Peters, that isn't *my* job!"

Travis had been doing some fast thinking. This deputy was no fool, and if the big man who had killed the Kansas Kid *was* Codine, he just might be able to convince Mido Peters of that fact. But jailing the bounty hunter was not the solution.

"It's not your job, either, Sheriff," Travis said quietly. "It's mine." He shrugged, turned on a wry grin. "Still, I think we're both right in taking this slow. I'm not *sure* that the big fellow is Ben Codine."

"He may be," Peters put in grimly, glad to be taken off the hook. "But if he is, where are the others? From what I've been reading, Ben Codine is no longer riding alone?"

Shaney started to say something, but Travis flicked him a warning look. "That's what I've been thinking," he said. "Codine didn't come to Labelle to spend the winter. He and his men have something cooked up. What?"

"One hundred and fifty-five thousand dollars!" Peters muttered uneasily, "arriving by special train on New Year's Day."

Travis hid the swift gleam of avarice that flickered in his eyes. "If he's the bounty hunter I'm looking for, then that's what he's after, Peters. And we'll give him just enough rope, this time, to hang himself!"

Ben Codine walked through the crowded lobby of the Baker House and went upstairs to the room he had signed for. He left his gear and came back downstairs and killed time at the barbershop where a hot bath took the chill from him, and the barber clipped shaggy hair and shaved the black stubble from his face.

He picked up a condensed history of Labelle while sitting in the barber's chair, and he learned all that was worth knowing about Jake Grady and the coming New Year's Eve celebration. The man added an item of gossip which caught Ben's interest. Something about a surprise Jake Grady was planning for his employees, but the barber didn't know just what the surprise was.

Ben's thoughts drifted back to the Kid. He was pretty sure the Kid was with Flint, and that Flint would soon know that Ben was in Labelle. The outlaw would do one of several things: he could come after Ben, run, or lay low.

The bounty hunter had a hunch that Ira would lay low. The killer had not come to Labelle for his health. Ira had something planned here, and even Ben's showing up would not frighten him away.

But it did mean that Ben would have to be on his guard. He knew the risks he was running. There were posters tacked up in parts of Texas and the Territory now, with a thousand-dollar reward for him, dead or alive. It was an irony of fate that he was now the hunted, that the bounty was on *his* head.

Ben still carried Sheriff Tolliver's letter in his boot, but he wondered, if he ever got cornered, what credence Mido Peters would put on this recommendation.

He made the rounds of the saloons, listening and watching. By nightfall he was convinced that Ira Flint was not in town. He saw Peters once, in his rounds; the deputy sheriff made no attempt to talk to him. He ran across a couple of young men wearing badges; they, too, gave him a wide berth.

No one seemed to know the Kansas Kid here in Labelle and Ben heard little talk about the shooting, which did not surprise him. In the midst of celebration, the shooting between two strangers did not merit much attention.

He remembered Mrs. Buskin's invitation as he was heading back for the hotel and he turned up the quiet side street to the white-painted house.

Aline met him at the door. There was a shine to her eyes as she led him into the warm living room.

"Ben, you've met my mother?"

Mary Buskin nodded pleasantly to him from the kitchen. Her brother appeared in the doorway, eyeing Ben with shiny admiration.

"And my brother, Tommy."

Ben nodded to the boy who started to come toward him but was pulled back into the kitchen by his mother. "I need your help here, young man," Mary said sternly. She didn't, really, but she didn't want Tommy intruding between Aline and Ben.

Harvey Buskin rose as they went into the front room, the town newspaper in his hand. Aline said: "And my father, Harvey. This is Mr. Codine, Father."

Ben smiled warmly: "First man I met coming into Labelle," he told Aline. He felt the older man's hand clasp his strongly.

"Aline told me what happened on the way in to town," Harvey said. "I'm glad you didn't hang around to talk too long, up at my shack." His eyes were studying Ben; the clean-shaven face, the grave eyes, and he liked what he saw. "Well, now that we know each other, Ben," he said, "let's eat. I'm hungry."

They sat around a large round table in the kitchen where the range lids glowed red hot and a comfortable warmth enfolded them. The chicken dumplings were all that Mary Buskin had promised.

At the end of the meal, over apple pie and coffee, Ben eased the conversation around to Harvey's work. "Long ride back and forth," he said. "Do it every day?"

Harvey nodded. "I take the handcar. There's a grade going out, but I coast most of the way in." Buskin had his pipe going now. "Shack's built at the old Lucky Try cutoff. Used to be a day and night shift then, to shunt loaders onto the spur. Now. . . ." He shrugged. "I don't do much. Keep an eye on the condition of the track up by the Gap, look for loose rails, fallen rock."

"Reckon you'll be spending the New Year home, then?" Ben said, making conversation.

Harvey shrugged. "No. There's a special

train coming through the Gap about eight-thirty." He lifted his hand to the pipe bowl and changed the subject with gruff abruptness, his eyes frowning a barely discernible warning to his wife and daughter.

"You a mining man, Ben?"

"Did a little panning once," Ben replied. "Worked a claim with a partner, in the Panamints. I lost fifteen pounds and a grubstake." He shrugged. "After that I sort of got shuffled into another line of business."

There was an uncomfortable pause while they waited for him to elaborate. Ben glanced up at the wall clock. "I really must be going," he said. He looked across to Mrs. Buskin as he rose. "Thanks for the chicken dumplings, ma'am. It was all you said it would be."

Mary Buskin glanced at her daughter and reacted to the edge of disappointment she saw in Aline's eyes. She smiled at Ben. "Tomorrow is New Year's Eve. We'd love to have you stay and see the old year out with us, Ben."

Ben looked at her. Out of the corner of his eyes he saw Aline lean slightly forward, waiting.

New Year's Eve . . . a time for gladness . . . and a time for reflection. He had lived a life with a woman . . . lived it and looked forward to a future. He took a deep breath, shaking the old memories from him. It wouldn't be fair to a girl like Aline . . . he was just a stranger, just someone passing through.

Harvey Buskin got to his feet, tamping tobacco into his pipe bowl. Harvey was a deliberate man who was slow to make judgments about people, and careful in his loyalties. But he was making a judgment now, indicating it in the tone of his voice.

"Labelle's a growing town, Ben, with lots of opportunities for a young man. I could talk to the Santa Fe superintendent."

Ben nodded. "Thank you, Mr. Buskin. But I'm in town on some other business. Once it's concluded, I don't expect to stay."

Aline walked with him to the door. She was disappointed, but she tried to hide it.

"You will come again, Ben. Before you leave?"

Ben nodded. "I'll see you."

Aline remained in the doorway, watching him stride down the path to the gate, turn up the street. Behind her, in the kitchen, Harvey Buskin puffed quietly on his pipe. Mary Buskin started slowly to take away the dishes.

"Don't push too hard, Mary," Harvey said.

His wife looked at him, a quiet bitterness in her eyes. Neither she nor Harvey were aware that Tommy was in the doorway of his room, listening.

"She's twenty-three years old," Mary said.

"You know what that means out here for a girl?"

Harvey shrugged. "She's been asked."

"By a half dozen men, including that nice clerk in Ed Rascomb's store." She glanced toward the door, hidden by an ell, where Aline had gone with Ben. "She's too choosy, Harvey." She turned back to her husband, a sad smile wrinkling her lips. "That's what too much book reading does to a young girl; she grows up with romantic notions." Mary's head shook slowly, compassion showing fleetingly in her eyes. "When I was a girl these things were arranged much more practically."

Harvey eyed her quizzically. "I remember," he said slowly. "You ran away to marry me." He smiled. "It hasn't been too bad, has it, Mary?"

Mary took a deep breath. "Maybe we were lucky. And I was eighteen." Her gaze went back to that unseen front door. "She's five years older, and all she can do now is wait." She turned to the sink with her dishes. "That's all any woman can do, is wait."

Travis Paine dismounted in the JD yard and grinned stiffly at the shadowy figure who came out of the barn holding cocked rifle.

"Damn cold ride, Wally," Travis greeted him. "Ira inside?"

Wally nodded. "What brings you out here?"

"The Kid," Travis replied, and turned to the door. He had followed Paul Shaney's directions to the JD; he had to let Ira know what had happened to the Kid.

Flint and Monk Ulley were playing cards in front of the pot-bellied heater. Jesse Dodd was in a corner, working on some old harness. He looked like some dog that had been kicked and beaten and was grateful for this moment of being left alone.

Martha Dodd was in her daughter's bedroom. She spent most of her time there, except when she emerged to cook meals for these demanding men.

Flint turned his head to look as Travis and Wally came inside. He reacted to Paine's appearance with quick, frowning surprise. He stood up, tossing his hand down.

"What brings you up here, Travis? Where's the Kid?"

"The Kid's dead!" Travis replied bluntly. He repeated what had happened, as he knew it. "A big hombre, about your size and build, Ira. Could be a dead ringer for you, only his beard is black and his hair isn't dyed. Claimed he found the black stud running loose outside of town and brought him in." Travis shrugged. "The Kid must have recognized the stud as the one that got away from you, Ira. He and this big fellow had words, and the Kid got it," he added coldly, hammering at the disbelief in Ira's eyes. "The Kid died with a gun

89

in his hand, Ira. I saw it!"

"*Codine!*" The name burst from Wally's lips. He was standing behind Ira, rifle held in the crook of his arm.

As Ira whirled to him: "The one chance in a million," Wally said grimly, "but Ben Codine made it!"

For a moment after his outburst there was a shocked, intense silence in the room. Even Jesse Dodd seemed caught up in it. He stopped working on the old harness and eyed them, a guarded curiosity in his eyes.

The bleakness in the blond outlaw's eyes faded slowly; he began to chuckle. A grim, flinty sound that held no mirth, only a cruel note of anticipation.

"All right, Wally — so Ben Codine's alive! And he's here looking for me!"

The others stared at him. Wally's whisper was a ragged condemnation. "Have you gone crazy, Ira? You know what his showing up here at this time means? He's found that big wild stud of his; he knows you're holed out somewhere. So he runs into the Kid and pushes him and then kills him."

"He's guessing," Travis cut in coldly. "He doesn't know about this place. He doesn't suspect me. And that deputy sheriff in town is on my side. Give me any excuse and I could put a slug into Codine and probably get a pat on the back from Mido Peters."

Flint smashed a fist into his open palm.

"We'll do better than that, Travis. We'll give him Ben Codine, bounty hunter turned outlaw, right after the holdup. Only this time it'll be the real Ben Codine!"

Travis frowned. Wally kept shaking his head. He had lived with the uneasy thought of this for too long a time; it had been a mistake to leave a man as dangerous as Codine alive, even if it had seemed impossible that he could have lasted the night with that bullet in him.

"Let's clear out of here, Ira," he snapped. "While the getting's good."

Flint ignored him. "A couple of hundred drunken miners shouldn't be too hard to convince, Travis," he said. "Especially when it's their money Ben Codine is after."

Travis was following Ira up to a point. "Won't be hard to whip them into a lynching mob," he agreed. "But what about Ben?"

"He'll be waiting for you and that mob," Flint sneered. "With a bullet in his legs. Up by the Lucky Try switchoff at Silver Gap —"

"Wait a minute," Monk growled. "I got lost somewhere. How do we get Ben Codine up there?"

Flint looked at Monk. "He's looking for a man who rode that big black stud of his. He wants me, Monk, he wants me so bad I'm figuring he'll swallow the bait we'll hold out to him."

He turned back to Paine. "There's a shack

91

down by Conner Creek, just behind this valley. I used to go there when I was a kid. . . ." He kept talking, the others moving closer to listen.

When he finished Wally shook his head. "It's too risky, Ira. You slipped up once on him. Don't take another chance."

Flint turned an impatient scowl on the little man. "You can pull out of this right now, if you feel that way, Wally!"

Wally caught the flare of cruelty in the man's eyes and he shrugged. "I'm staying." His voice fell to a low mutter. "But I think you're gonna live just long enough to regret it, Ira."

VIII

Tommy Buskin stood on the corner of Lode-stone Avenue and Main and felt the bite of the icy night wind tingle his cheeks. He was out after dark and he knew he would catch hell when he got back home, but it was almost the end of the year and, what the heck! a fourteen-year-old boy was almost a man, wasn't he?

He moved to the edge of the walk and watched the men and women who thronged by. Many of them were in from outlying farms, some for last-minute shopping before returning home. Labelle had become a sort of mecca for this entire corner of the Territory, thanks to Jake Grady.

Yet despite its booming quality Labelle was not a raw frontier town. It had passed through its wild stage during the first gold strike, and now there was a settled quality to the mining town, marked by the small rail-road depot and the big stone and brick building, four stories high, that housed the Stockmen & Miners Bank on the first floor and professional offices above.

Tommy turned to look down the wide, shadowy street to the distant, snow-mantled hills. There was a charged excitement in the boy that was sparked by the sounds of early revelry coming from inside the saloons and the hurrying passersby. But it was the big-hatted men riding into Labelle on sleek, mettlesome horses that most caught his interest. They were silent men, usually, tall and lean and seemingly born in the saddle. For Tommy they carried the aura of distant places, of warmer lands to the south, of adventure.

Some day he'd leave Labelle and ride south, some day he, too, would wear a gun on his hip like the big man who had come to supper tonight.

A buckboard rolled into town, its seats crammed with young men in starched collars and stiff Sunday-best clothes. One of them slid a rifle from under the seat and fired it into the air, adding a wild Yahoooo! on the heels of the fading shots. The wagon was immediately hauled to one side of the street by Mido Peters' two special deputies and the rifle confiscated, as a precaution.

Tommy cut across the street and dodged between two incoming riders to make the plankwalk on the other side. He heard a man's deep voice call out goodnaturedly: "Better watch it, kid," and he turned and looked back, feeling somehow accepted and part of Labelle's celebrating throng tonight.

He started to drift aimlessly, peering into darkened shop windows, turning to eye each new wagon that rolled by. Once one of Mido's deputies, coming out of a saloon, paused to study him briefly, then walked on.

Midway down the block the flaring torches of the Silver Queen Saloon splashed their lurid glow across the walk. The Silver Queen was Labelle's gaudiest and wildest night spot and the batwings creaked back and forth to the coming and going of its customers. From inside welled a rough medley of music, whiskey-hoarse male voices, and high, thin laughter of its women entertainers.

Tommy swung toward it and stopped suddenly, eyeing the head framed against the big lamp-lighted window. He knew that head and the frayed-bill cap pulled down over cold ears and a surge of warmth went through him. He called: "Rick!"

The boy at the window turned quickly and lamplight, falling across his sharp face, revealed freckled features, wide eyes and a snub of a nose. Rick Myles sat behind Tommy in school; they shared pencils, erasers, lunch and forbidden "penny dreadfuls," lurid paper-covered tales of the wild West. Rick's mother was dead; his father worked in the Grady mine. A spinster aunt took care of him.

Rick eyed Tommy with shamefaced relief. "Gee, you're out, too?" he said and glanced past Tommy, down the walk, as if half expecting to see Tommy's sister coming after him.

Tommy shrugged. "Sure," he said casually, implying he had permission. "It's New Year's Eve, ain't it?" He glanced toward the brightly-lighted window of the Silver Queen. "What's going on inside?"

Rick grinned shyly. "Can't see much, but they're sure making a lot of noise."

The big, life-size poster tacked to the building wall to left of the batwing doors advertised a buxom, high-kicking dancing girl, one of a "dozen girls specially imported from Denver's music hall." Tommy pressed up close to the window, but all he could make out was a blur of men at tables, clapping hands to the tune of *Clementine*, and a glimpse of a chorus line going through its routine on a small stage at the far end of the room.

A hard hand fell on his shoulder and Tommy stiffened as Mido Peters said, "That's a little too strong for you, Tommy," and he was pulled away from the window. Rick backed off and looked up at the deputy sheriff, ready to run.

Mido said sharply: "Go on home, both of you. Next time I see you on the streets I'll run you in!"

Tommy backed off and turned away. Rick jostled him as they started for the corner. They reached it, looked back. Mido was still standing in front of the Silver Queen, watching them. They ducked around the corner and walked quickly for a few steps, then Tommy stopped, a stubborn defiance in his face.

Rick looked at him, glanced back to the corner. "I think we better go home," he said.

Tommy shook his head. "You can go if you're afraid." He started off down the side street. Rick ran to catch up with him. "I sneaked out the bedroom window. My Pa'll skin me alive, when he finds out."

Tommy kept walking. Rick paced him for a spell, then: "Where we going?"

"Rio Vegas' stables."

They cut down an alley and came out on a quiet back street and turned in toward the sign that proclaimed VEGAS LIVERY STABLES.

The big barn door at the head of the small ramp was closed, but a light spilled out through a narrow side window. Tommy peered inside, then swung back to the door and made a motion for Rick to give him a hand.

Rick hung back. "Rio's got a mean temper, Tommy. If he finds us foolin' around inside. . . ."

Tommy cut him off. "The old man ain't inside, he must be out to supper. Come on, we won't be long."

They slid the big door back, making an opening just wide enough for them to slip inside. A lantern, wick turned down, hung on a nail on a center post. The stalls were full, the air warm and close with the smell of horses. Iron shod hoofs thumped restlessly on floor boards.

Tommy turned to Rick. "Sis said it was a big black stallion."

They moved along the stalls, stopping finally when they caught sight of Ben's big stud when it swung its head around to survey them from above the stall boards.

Rick stared up at the magnificent animal, awe gleaming in his eyes. "Boy he's big," he whispered. He moved up a little closer and the stallion snorted softly and shook his head and Rick stepped back quickly and looked at Tommy. "I bet he could lick a dozen —"

He choked off, suddenly aware of the limping figure behind Tommy. Tommy turned.

Rio Vegas paused, a toothpick jutting from a corner of his mouth. He eyed the two boys with a sternness he did not feel.

He growled: "Out a bit late, ain't you?"

Rick nodded jerkily. Tommy said brashly: "It ain't ten yet."

Vegas looked hard at him, sensing the edge of defiance in Tommy. It began early sometimes, he thought, the push to grow up. This boy needed a stronger guiding hand than his father's, or somewhere, soon, he would take a wrong turn.

Vegas said: "Could be your father's out looking for you right now."

Tommy shook his head. "Naw. Pa always goes to bed right after supper."

Vegas glanced at the big black stud in the stall behind the boys. He frowned. "What are you doing in here?"

"We wanted to see that wild horse that fought the wolves," Tommy answered. "The one that saved my sister this afternoon."

Vegas made a motion with his hand. "Better stay away from him," he said roughly. "That stallion's already caused the death of one man!"

Rick and Tommy turned to stare at the horse. "He *killed* somebody?"

Vegas shook his head impatiently. "Not the horse; the man who brought him in. Feller who calls himself Ben Smith. Another stranger came in here and claimed the stallion and Ben killed him."

"Gee!" Rick turned to Tommy, his eyes shining. But young Buskin was thinking of the big quiet man who had eaten supper with his family just a few hours ago and the way his sister Aline had looked at him.

"Why'd he do it, Mr. Vegas?" he asked.

Rio shook his head. "Two strangers fighting over a horse." He shrugged. "Gunmen, both of them. Can't tell what that kind is up to or what they fight about. But I sure hope that big feller moves on."

"You think there'll be more trouble?" Rick asked, eyes wide.

"There always is when you get men like that around," Rio said. He jerked a thumb toward the door. "Now the two of you skeedaddle out of here an' go on home, or I'll call Mido Peters!"

The boys backed out of the barn, reluctantly. Outside, Rick turned to Tommy. He scraped the toe of his worn shoe through the dirt, muttered: "Guess I'll go home, Tommy. It's getting late."

Tommy was staring off, toward the street. He didn't say anything.

Paul Shaney finished his drink at the Silver Queen bar and turned to eye Ben Codine pushing his way through the crowd for a place at the rail. He caught the big man's glance on him, cold and brief and sharply judging, and Shaney turned away, stiffening slightly to the prickles of fear that ran down the small of his back.

Damn Ira Flint! he reflected bitterly. Ira and his wild, show-off ideas! If he had killed Ben Codine when he had the chance. . . .

He pushed his empty glass aside and shook his head to the bartender who looked in his direction. His thoughts were still bitterly occupied with a development he had not foreseen when he had written to Ira Flint and asked him to come back to Labelle. He had not expected Ira would have a nemesis on his trail. But now Travis Paine had gone to see Ira and Ben Codine was prowling through Labelle like a tiger on an old spoor. And in this wild, pre-New Year's Eve crowd, anything could happen!

Paul reached inside his vest pocket for a cigar and it was then that the idea hit him. His hand trembled slightly as he lifted the smoke to his lips, for what he was thinking was murder and Paul Shaney was not a courageous man. He glanced over to Ben, covertly, but the bounty hunter's back was turned to him. Paul sucked in a deep breath and walked away from the bar, the cigar unlighted and forgotten.

Outside he glanced quickly up and down the dark, crowded street for a glimpse of Mido Peters, or someone who might recognize him. Not seeing anyone he knew, he crossed to the opposite walk and ducked quickly down an alley that brought him around to the back of the hotel. He paused briefly under the outside stairway, erected primarily as a means of escape for second floor occupants in case of fire. The stairs were seldom used.

The old wooden treads creaked as he went up. He waited on the landing, listening. Up here the hubbub from the main street was fainter; the stars shone crystal clear in the cold night sky.

He tried the back door and for a moment his spirits sank as it didn't budge. Sickeningly, he recalled that the door was bolted from inside. Then a flash of memory roused him. He had lived here for years and he knew the second floor of this hotel like the back of his hand. The small window next to the door, opening on the landing, was not secured.

Shaney worked quickly, trying to raise the sash. Weather had frozen it fast. Desperately, he took out his pocket knife and snapped the point of his blade, but he managed to pry it up far enough to get his fingers under it for leverage. The sash went up then, comparatively easy. Paul listened for a moment before sliding in across the sill. The hallway was dark and it was yet early enough so that all roomers were still out on the town, celebrating.

Paul carefully closed the window and turned to the back door. He eased the bolt back, tried the latch. The door opened easily. He breathed a sigh of relief as he closed it again.

His room was three doors down the hallway. He could be out of it and down these back stairs in thirty seconds.

He walked to his room, went inside, closed the door behind him. The room was dark, but he did not need a light to find his way around. He went first to the window, parted the old lace curtains, and very slowly, making no noise, he raised the sash.

The winter cold breathed into the room, flowing in from the distant, snow-capped hills. Paul turned quickly and walked to his closet. He reached inside, behind old clothes, for the rifle propped out of sight and against the closet wall. He had bought the Winchester to do some hunting a few years ago, but his interest had waned. He still had a box of shells for it somewhere.

He found the box under some old blankets folded on the top shelf in the closet. It was still more than half full. He started to dump the contents into his pockets, but then thought better of it. He would have time for one shot, perhaps two. He did not want to be caught, if luck ran against him, with rifle shells in his pocket.

He took two cartridges, dropped one into his coat pocket, inserted the other into place in the rifle. The box he replaced under the blankets.

He walked back to the window, stood by it, looking out. He had a good view of the front of the Silver Queen Saloon from here, but it was at an angle and across the street — a rather long and difficult shot for him. Still, he had no choice unless Ben, coming out, turned toward the corner.

It was then that Paul remembered the cigar still clenched between his teeth. He took it out of his mouth and slowly tucked it back into his vest pocket.

He didn't want smoke in his eyes when Ben Codine came out of the Silver Queen and into his gun sights!

IX

Ben Codine finished his second beer at the Silver Queen bar and said no to the bartender coming up to take his glass for a refill. He tossed a half dollar on the bar and drifted over toward the gaming tables.

A short-skirted, brightly-painted entertainer plucked at his elbow and smiled at him; Ben smiled back but there was no welcome in his eyes and she lost interest in him and went off, looking for a more agreeable companion.

This was the fourth bar Ben had visited since leaving the Buskin home. He was hoping he'd come across some clue to Ira's whereabouts, some casually or carelessly dropped word, some stranger, with a few drinks too many, saying something he shouldn't. But he had drawn a blank and Ben had the dismal feeling that he would learn nothing of Ira tonight. Even more depressing, it was quite possible that, hearing of the Kansas Kid's death, Ira had spooked and was even now a long way from Labelle.

The rough boisterousness of the crowd inside the saloon increased as the night wore on. A miner stumbled up from a blackjack game, cursing his rotten luck. His elbow jabbed into Ben crossing toward the doors.

He turned angrily, swinging blindly for Ben's face. Ben caught his arm, held him.

"Better luck next time," he said easily, and spun the miner around and out of his way. The man stared after him for a moment, then weaved his way to the bar.

Ben crossed to the batwings without further incident, then stepped out. The bite of the cold night wind was a welcome relief after the smoky closeness inside, and he paused to take a deep breath.

A miner, coming out behind him, jostled up against him. Ben stepped back and away from the doors and, across the street and unseen at his window, Paul Shaney cursed the miner as he slowly eased back on his trigger finger. He shifted slightly, his eyes squinting, trying to pick Ben up again. But the bounty hunter was a shadowy figure against the dark building line now, and Shaney eased, his eyes watchful. Ben would have to move out soon.

Coming up the street looking for her brother, Aline Buskin stopped as she saw Ben step out of the Silver Queen. His tall silhouette was easily recognizable in the light spilling through the saloon's batwings. Even after Ben moved out of the line of traffic, merging into the shadows, she watched him, a sharp feeling of discontent holding her.

Somehow she had thought Ben different from most of the men she had known — some quality in him, a quiet gentleness she sensed rather than observed — but he had declined to spend the evening with her family, obviously preferring the wilder pleasures of Labelle's night spots.

She shrugged slightly, telling herself it did not matter. After all, she hardly knew the man. She waited on the corner, preferring not to draw his attention, waiting for Ben to move on.

Behind her an early celebrator, two sheets to the wind and oblivious to all but a direct line to the Silver Queen, stumbled up against her. She turned quickly, tried to step back out of his way. But he reached out for her, a wide smile spreading across his face.

"Evenin', ma'am."

Aline tried to pull away from him, her cheeks burning, not so much from embarrassment at this accostment as from the thought Ben's attention might be drawn to her. But the drunk persisted.

"Pretty girl like you shouldn't be out alone."

"Please," Aline said, jerking free. "I . . . I'm waiting for someone."

He bowed in exaggerated courtesy. "Name's Jules," he said. "An' I'm here. Let me. . . ."

Aline stiffened as Ben's tall figure loomed up. She felt a bitter resentment at being put on a spot like this.

Ben put a hand on the drunk's shoulder,

faced him around. "Sorry, feller," he said quietly. "The lady's with me."

Jules backed off, surveyed Ben with owlish pugnacity. He was pretty drunk, but not so much so as not to understand the cold glint of danger in this tall man. He backed off, deciding there were greener and less harmful pastures elsewhere. He looked at Aline, wigwagged an apology with his hand. "No offense, ma'am."

He stumbled past them, weaving toward the Silver Queen, leaving Aline looking up at Ben, her eyes cool.

Ben said: "It's no night for a lady to be out without an escort. May I take you wherever you are going?"

"I'm not going anywhere," she said coldly. "I'm looking for my brother Tommy."

Ben eyed her briefly, the coldness in her voice not getting past him. He shrugged. "Boy his age could be anywhere." He smiled. "Let me help you look for him."

Aline shook her head. "Don't let me keep you from the pleasures inside the Silver Queen. I'm sure they're so much more interesting than —" she paused, then ended bitterly — "my family."

She started to walk past him, but he took hold of her arm and held her.

"I would have liked to stay," he said. "But I told you I had other business."

"In saloons?" She shrugged his hand off.

107

"Look, I know how you must have felt at dinner tonight." Her bitterness was tinged with shame. "I'm a schoolteacher, getting on in her years, and my father and mother hinted too much. Aline is unmarried, available to the first decent man who shows an interest in her." Her voice lifted angrily: "Well, it isn't true! I'm not up for sale."

"I never thought you were," Ben cut in gently. He took her arm. "Some day I may explain why —"

But Aline was still riding the crest of her bitterness. "You don't have to apologize. I *know* why you left!"

Ben cut in coldly: "Do you now?"

She started to walk away from him again, but this time he tightened his grip on her arm, swung her around. "Just what do you know about — ?"

He broke off and swung sharply around as Tommy's shrill voice cut at him: "Leave my sister alone!"

Tommy had just rounded the corner. He ran toward Ben and Aline, wedging himself in between them. And in that moment, Paul Shaney took a chance and fired. . . .

Tommy spun around and fell and Aline stood petrified, staring over Tommy's body, across the street, not really seeing anything, just too shocked to move.

Ben lunged for her just as the second rifle shot smashed the glass of the darkened shop window behind him. And it was in that split second that he realized whoever was doing the shooting was trying *for him!*

He pulled Aline down and back within the partial protection of the darkened doorway and his holster gun was out in that one quick movement. His eyes searched the hotel across the street. He knew only that the shots had come from there — *they had to!*

Aline fought the terror inside her. "Tommy!" she screamed and tried to move past Ben, to her brother, moaning softly on the walk.

Hurrying figures moved toward them. Ben eased out as men formed a partial screen around them, around Tommy. He pushed through them, and with Aline he knelt beside the boy. He put a hand down on the boy and reacted to the warm blood under his fingers.

Aline looked at him, her heart in her throat. "How is he?"

"Bullet hit his left arm, but I think it missed the bone." At the stricken look in Aline's face: "He'll be all right. Get him home, get a doctor!"

There was a press of men and women around them now. Through them elbowed Mido Peters. The gaunt deputy sheriff looked down at them, stiffening at the sight of Ben. His right hand drew back to his holstered gun, hooked there.

He looked directly at Ben Codine. "What

happened?" he asked coldly.

"Somebody got careless with a rifle," Ben answered grimly. "He hit the boy."

Mido shifted his attention to Aline. She was bent over her brother, concerned about him.

Mido said: "Is that right, Aline?"

She looked up at him, nodded impatiently. "I was here, talking with Ben. Tommy came running up and —" She looked past Mido. "I think the shots came from the hotel."

Mido frowned.

"Tommy," Aline said bitterly. "Who would want to hurt him? He's only a boy."

Mido's gaze went back to Ben. He *knew* it wasn't Tommy the ambusher had been after! And yet — *who?*

Ben, in the meantime, had knotted his handkerchief in makeshift tourniquet over the bullet wound in Tommy's arm. He helped Tommy to his feet.

"Can you walk?" he asked the boy.

Tommy nodded. Even in the dim light here Ben could see his white, frightened face. He turned to Aline. "Get him home and in bed. I'll be by a little later."

She nodded numbly. Tommy leaned against her. The crowd parted to let them through.

Ben started to cut across the street but was stopped by the deputy sheriff. "I'll go with you," Peters said grimly.

The hotel lobby held a scattering of loungers, mostly people waiting around for someone else. The clerk behind the desk looked harried. He shook his head to Mido's question.

"Rifle shots? No, I didn't hear anything." He threw up his hands. "With all the commotion in town tonight. . . ."

"They came from the hotel — from somewhere upstairs," Ben said grimly.

The clerk looked at him. "I didn't hear anything." He looked at Peters. "I've been busy. And there's been shots, off and on, all night. Haven't really been paying much attention."

"You register any strangers lately?" Ben put in quietly. "Someone for an outside room, overlooking the street?"

The clerk shrugged. "All outside rooms are occupied by our old tenants." He paused. "You and Mister Travis Paine are the only strangers to check in within the past week."

Ben frowned. "Where is Mister Paine?"

"He left this afternoon," the clerk replied. "Said he'd be gone the rest of the day. Mister Paine kept his room, said he'd be back tomorrow. He didn't want to miss the celebration."

Mido looked at Ben. "I'll vouch for Travis Paine," he said coldly.

He glanced at Paul Shaney, just coming into the hotel lobby. The Grady bookkeeper had a cigar stuck in his mouth. He looked like a man who had had a few drinks and was in cheerful mood. He crossed toward the desk.

"Hello, Peters." He glanced at Ben, his curiosity veiled as though he was seeing Ben for the first time. He said, offhandedly: "Trying to talk Nate into giving up a room for a friend, Sheriff?"

Mido said bleakly: "No."

He turned to Ben, his eyes hard, unfriendly. "Those shots weren't meant for Tommy Buskin," he said coldly. "Too bad the kid happened to get in the way." His eyes measured Ben. "I won't turn a man out on the trail on a cold night like this, mister, not even you. But I'm repeating: you clear out of Labelle tomorrow, or I'll find a place for you — in a cell!"

He turned on his heel, strode out. Ben looked after him, his eyes thoughtful. Then his gaze swung around to Paul Shaney.

Paul's teeth tightened on the soggy end of his cigar. He said: "Mido Peters is sure on the prod tonight, Mister. Wonder what happened?"

Ben didn't answer him. He knew he'd find nothing, even if he tried to force a search of the rooms upstairs. And Mido, by his cold dismissal of the affair, made it impossible for him even to try.

He eyed the desk clerk. "Mister Paine say where he was going?"

The clerk shook his head. "On some business, I gathered." He turned slowly and watched Ben leave, then his gaze swung around to Paul Shaney.

"What happened out there, Mr. Shaney? Somebody get hurt?"

Paul shrugged. "I thought it was just someone taking a few pot shots at the stars." He turned to the stairs, keeping his walk unhurried. He didn't want to draw attention to himself. But he had to get to the back door and bolt it, before anyone noticed.

The doctor was just about finished bandaging Tommy's arm when Ben Codine knocked on the door and Aline let him inside. Mrs. Buskin and her husband, Harvey, in nightshirt and robe and still sleepy-eyed, were in Tommy's room. Tommy looked better, the shock having worn off and only the pain in his arm bothering him now. He already had the sullen look of a boy who had been scolded when Ben and Aline came into the bedroom.

The doctor snapped his medical bag shut, turned to Mary Buskin. He held out a small envelope. "Give him two of these with a glass of water. It'll help him sleep tonight. Check the bandages in the morning. I'll be around as soon as I can." He picked up his bag, turned to the door.

"Don't know how many dern fools will shoot themselves before the year's out."

He glanced at Ben, smiled at Aline, as he

went out. Harvey moved up to the head of the bed and glowered down at his son.

"I ought to take a strap to you, anyway," he growled. "Sneaking out and roaming the streets, this time of night!" He turned to Ben. "Don't know what's come over the boy, lately. Last year he wouldn't have dreamed of doing a fool thing like this."

"Your son's growing up," Ben said quietly. He looked down at Tommy and the boy returned his look, a hostile light in his eyes and Ben frowned, wondering why.

"Seen enough of the bright lights?" he smiled.

Tommy's gaze shifted to Aline. He said sullenly: "I was coming home, sis. You didn't have to come out looking for me!"

"Now see here, son!" Harvey growled. "Don't you go talking to your sister like that! If I had come after you —"

"Oh, leave the boy alone!" his wife said, cutting between Harvey and the bed. "You can scold him later, when he's feeling better."

She looked at Ben and Aline. "I'll stay with Tommy." To her husband, she said: "Why don't you invite Mister . . ." her eyes went to Ben. "Why don't you all go into the kitchen and have a drink?" She turned back to her husband. "I think we still have a bottle of whiskey, the one you keep for colds?"

Harvey nodded. He led the way to the kitchen, crossed to the cupboard, took down a half-filled bottle. He turned to Ben.

"Thanks," Ben declined. "But not for me, not tonight."

"You don't drink?"

Ben shrugged. "Like any other man. But I've had all I want tonight."

Harvey took the bottle to the kitchen table anyway. "I can stand a nip," he muttered. He looked at his daughter. "How's the coffee?"

"Still warm," Aline said. She looked at Ben, her eyes still holding him off. "Would you like a cup?"

Ben nodded, his curiosity holding him. "Never found it bothered my sleep any."

He sat down across the table from Harvey, who brought his pipe from the stove shelf where he had left it. There was tobacco still in the bowl and he lighted up, absently, out of habit.

"Fool kid," he grumbled as Aline poured coffee. "Could of gotten himself killed." He pulled the cork from the whiskey bottle, poured a generous slug of it into his coffee. "Whole town's full of drunks." He reached for the sugar bowl, spooned two generous measures into his cup and stirred.

"Try some in your coffee," he suggested to Ben. "Makes a great nightcap. Eyetalian worker on the railroad started me using it. I think they call it a coffee royal."

Ben said: "I'll stick to it straight." He grinned a little. "It's not the whiskey or the coffee; it's the sugar I mind."

He drank his coffee, glanced up at Aline. "I am keeping you up," he said. "I'm glad Tommy's all right."

He got to his feet. "If I have a chance, I'll drop by tomorrow."

"I'll be up at the switchoff," Harvey said. "But you're welcome here. Come any time."

Ben turned to Aline. "Good night."

"I'll see you to the door," she said. Now that he was going the coldness in her knotted in a tight ball inside her. She hated herself for what she felt for this man, but she couldn't help it.

She stopped outside on the porch with him. He looked at her for a moment, nodded, turned to go. She took a step after him.

"Ben!"

He turned. She said nothing further, but there was a look in her eyes that brought him back to her. "Don't go, Ben."

He felt the pull of her appeal, and then reaction set in. He shook his head. "Don't wait for me, Aline. Not for me. There must be other men."

"Not like you, Ben." Her eyes had a bitter shine to them. "Don't go."

Ben took a long breath. "Why, Aline? What do you know about me?" His voice held a bleak distaste. "I'm just a man who happened by at the right time to help you. I could be

116

anybody, a man running from the law. A man with a wife and children."

"No!" Her voice was small, but firm. "I don't believe it, Ben. But . . . if it were true. . . ." She moved up close to him. "If it were, Ben, I wouldn't care. I wouldn't care!"

Her face was lifted up to him, her eyes searching his face, and all the long years since his wife's death suddenly crowded into one great ball of loneliness in Ben. He took her into his arms and kissed her.

When he finally stepped back he was a man at peace with himself. He smiled: "Aline, I'll be back. No matter what happens I'll be back for you."

He turned then, walked away, and Aline's eyes followed him until he was lost in the cold dark shadows. Then she went back into the house.

X

The last day of the year dawned with clearing skies and rising temperatures, as though it wanted to be remembered kindly. The merriment in Labelle was starting early. Punchers from the big ranches on the Flats began drifting in, joining the crowds in the hotel bar and saloons.

Ben came down into the lobby of the Baker House where a big table had been set up in the middle of the floor holding a huge punch bowl, and attended by a smiling Negro who handed out drinks on "Mistah Grady, suh."

The bounty hunter paused for a drink. He didn't see Travis until the man pushed up beside him.

The phony U.S. Marshal said quietly: "Heard you were looking for me last night?"

Ben glanced at him. Paine's eyes were cold and told him nothing. He shrugged, checking the first faint surge of suspicion concerning this man.

"Someone took a shot at me from the hotel . . . from one of the windows facing the street."

"Me?" Travis' voice was bleak.

Ben shook his head. "If it had been you,

you wouldn't have missed."

"Thanks," Travis said drily. He found a cup in his hand, put there by the Negro servant, and he turned to Ben, a thin smile on his lips.

"Heard you're looking for the man who lost that big black stud you found yesterday?"

Ben eyed the man, searching his face, but he could see only a grim seriousness in the man's eyes.

He nodded, holding back the surge of interest in him. "What about it?"

The fake U.S. Marshal indicated a comparatively quiet corner of the lobby. Ben followed him to it.

"I rode into Labelle two nights ago," Travis said, keeping his voice down. "Took a short cut I knew, along a small creek bed. That's when I first saw that black stallion of yours. Wild as a mustang. I couldn't get near him. It was getting dark and a storm was brewing. But I saw tracks of a man on foot, right after, heading toward a shack. There was smoke coming out of the chimney, and at the time I remember thinking someone had holed up in there."

Ben's voice was hard. "Why are you telling me?"

Travis kept his voice even. "Because I'm figuring we're both after the same man. Ben Codine!"

Ben kept his eyes neutral; he said slowly:

119

"The bounty hunter, Marshal?"

Travis nodded. "I received a tip he was headed this way. I didn't give much thought to that shack, until I heard what happened in the Vegas stables and I had a talk with Rio. That shack's been deserted for years. I've got a hunch that wild stud threw Codine, and being on foot he had to hole up there. Might be he's waiting for other members of his bunch to rendezvous with him."

It made sense to Ben. It was a lead, however slim, the only lead Ben had run into so far that might lead him to Ira Flint. But the thin finger of caution touched the bounty hunter.

"Why tell me, Marshal? He's *your* man."

Paine's lips curled. "I heard the stableman tell how you gunned down the Kansas Kid." He nodded at the glint that flashed in Ben's eyes. "Sure, I recognized him. But it wouldn't do any good telling that deputy sheriff, Peters. He'd probably panic if he knew Ben Codine was around. I want to get Codine. But I'll be honest with you. I know his reputation and I don't fancy taking him alone." He eyed Ben briefly. "You were good enough to gun down the Kid, now are you willing to take a chance on that outlaw bounty hunter? For half of a ten-thousand-dollar reward?"

The irony of this appealed to Ben. "Sure," he murmured. "I'll take the chance."

He had promised to see Aline and look in on Tommy, but at this moment he forgot them. He followed Travis Paine out of the lobby to the stables for his horse.

The Conner Creek shack stood back a few yards from the icy stream, a squat wooden structure beginning to sag with age. A rusted piece of stovepipe jutted from the wall to the right of the door, but no smoke came from it. The door was closed.

Travis frowned. "Looks like he cleared out." His voice held the thin edge of disappointment. "I came by here last night. I could have sworn I spotted smoke out of that stovepipe."

Ben surveyed the shack. It looked innocent enough, but some vague warning stirred in him. He did not protest when the man beside him said: "You cover me. I'll ride up and take a look."

Nig shook his head, jingling bit irons. Rested and fed, the black stallion was showing his pleasure at being with Ben again.

Codine watched Travis ride slowly toward that closed door. There was no window facing him, and there was not enough cover around to hide anyone. The thirty foot ridge of gray, snow-covered rock was too far away even for a good rifleman. But there was something wrong about this whole thing, and Ben sensed it. He kept his eye on that closed door, his rifle held easily across his saddle.

Paine dismounted and walked to the shack front and stood by that door, holding his rifle ready. He gave the door a kick and jumped back, waiting.

There was no movement, nor did the door open. Paine shot a glance back to Ben and made a motion with his shoulders, indicating disappointment. Then he reached for the latch, shoved the door inward, and followed the muzzle of his rifle inside.

He was gone out of Ben's sight only a moment. Then he stepped out and waved to Ben to join him, shaking his head.

The bounty hunter rode up. "Somebody was here, all right," Paine growled. "But he may have spotted my tracks out there last night and pulled out."

Ben dismounted, leaving Nig beside Travis' gray mare. He walked to the door. Something smelled wrong. His glance picked up boot prints in the hard-packed snow, moving away from the shack, toward the creek. He was at the door when the pattern made its sharp warning in his head.

He was a split second too late!

Travis' rifle muzzle jabbed lightly against the small of his back, then withdrew. "Step inside, Codine!"

A tall dark figure appeared within the cabin, in line with the door, echoing Paine's order. "Come in, Ben."

Codine's gaze touched the gun in Ira Flint's hand, lifted to the sneer on the outlaw's face.

He had walked into as smooth a trap as any he had encountered; he probably would not live to make this mistake again.

"You've got a gun in your hand now, like you wanted," Ben said evenly. "You still think you're the better man?"

Ira laughed. "That slug Wally put into you didn't affect your guts, Ben. But I have a better idea. You said you'd see me hang, remember?" He chuckled. "That's what I'm going to see happen to you, Codine; I'm going to see that you hang high!"

Ben stiffened as Travis' rifle muzzle touched his back again. The phony Marshal's voice was flat. "Shuck that gunbelt, and do it right!"

Ben's fingers loosened his belt; he let it fall at his feet.

A hulking figure appeared beside Flint, pushing slightly ahead of the outlaw to face Ben. Small bright eyes raked Ben in hard appraisal.

"So this is the big he-rooster who's got Wally shaking in his boots?" Monk spat deliberately on Ben's boot. Then his right hand came up in a flat-palmed smash against Codine's cheek. He stepped in quickly and brought his knee up for Ben Codine's groin.

Ben twisted just enough to catch the blow on his hip; his own right hand smash spun

Monk around, back into Ira. The big man's knees momentarily wobbled. . . .

"Hold it!" Flint snarled, shoving Monk away from him. "You can have all the fun you want with him later, as long as you keep him alive." He looked at Ben, a mocking glint in his eyes. "Until tomorrow, at eight-thirty!"

All morning Aline Buskin had tried to suppress her eagerness at Ben's coming from her mother. Tommy was doing fine, lying in bed, being catered to by his mother. Harvey had left early for the shack at Silver Spur Gap.

But as the morning wore on and Ben did not appear she felt the weight of her mother's silent looks, and her spirits sank. She walked to the window for the dozenth time and Mary Buskin, coming out of Tommy's room, said quietly: "Tommy wants to see you, Aline."

She turned and went into the bedroom and her mother remained outside. Tommy was hitched up on his pillow, his arm bandaged, his freckles more prominent against the paleness of his face. He had a cup of hot chocolate on the table beside him, a book face down on the covers by his feet.

Aline glanced at the title: *Gulliver's Travels*. She smiled at him. "Good way to end the old year, Tommy, catching up on your school work."

He eyed her solemnly. "You like him, sis?"

Aline felt her cheeks burn. "Who?"

"Ben."

She smiled, hiding her inner confusion. "Why, of course, Tommy. He saved my life."

"Really like him?" Tommy was blunt. "You want to marry him?"

Aline stared at him. "Why, what a thing to ask." He looked at her, waiting. She moved closer to the bed. "Yes," she said softly. "Yes . . . I'd marry him. If he asked me."

Tommy's good hand reached out for hers. "I . . . I like him, too, Sis, but he killed a man in Rio's stables." Aline's eyes widened. "Rio told us . . . me an' Rick. We were there last night . . . wanted to see that big black horse." Tommy took a breath. "Rio thinks Ben ain't his real name; he thinks he's an outlaw."

Aline's fingers tightened on Tommy's. She smiled, her smile a little forced. "I don't care," she whispered, "I don't care." She bent over and kissed him and left the room.

Her mother was waiting in the kitchen. She was curious. "What did Tommy want?"

Aline shook her head. It was not the time to talk of Ben with her mother, not now. She went into her room for her coat and mittens and came back into the kitchen.

"I think I'll drive up and visit with the Dodds," she said. "I haven't seen Theresa since Christmas, and I know she wasn't feeling well. I'll be back before it gets dark."

Mary Buskin nodded. She was an understanding woman, and she sensed her daughter's disappointment in Ben's not coming. "I wish Tommy was well enough to ride with you," she said. "After what happened, I'd feel better knowing someone was with you."

"I don't think I'll have that sort of trouble again, Mother," Aline reassured. "And I promise not to stay long."

She stopped at the livery for the buggy and while Vegas harnessed up, her glance searched the stalls. She spotted the roan mare Ben had ridden into town, but the big black stallion was gone.

Vegas caught her glance. He said: "That feller, Ben, left this morning. With that U.S. Marshal who just showed up in town, a feller name of Travis Paine."

Aline smiled. "I was just curious." But she felt the wave of embarrassment at the look Rio Vegas gave her.

She drove through Labelle's busy streets and felt better only when the town was behind her. She knew it couldn't be true, but she felt that all of Labelle knew of her feelings for the tall stranger named Ben and was secretly laughing at her.

"I've got to get over this," she told herself. "I'm behaving like a school girl."

It was past noon when she turned the buggy into the JD ranch yard.

The door opened while she was still in the buggy seat. A small, wiry man she had never seen before stepped out of the house. He carried a rifle in the crook of his arm and as he surveyed her he said, drily: "You lookin' for somebody, Miss?"

Aline sat still, not understanding. The Dodds may have hired a hand. She nodded slowly. "Why, yes. I've come to see Theresa Dodd. Who are you?"

Wally grinned. "A guest, Miss. Step right down an' come inside."

She hesitated, sensing something wrong. There was no sign of the Dodds; usually they met her at the door, glad to see her. They seldom had visitors. But the house seemed strangely quiet, unfestive. Even Buff, the Dodd dog, was nowhere in sight.

She caught the small man's eyes as they went past her and she turned to follow his glance.

Two men were riding into the ranchyard. One was a stranger she didn't recognize, the other looked like Ben, and her heart leaped. But as they drew closer she saw it was not Ben, although the resemblance in body build was remarkable. But the man's face, showing a sprouting of a blond beard, was too hard and the mouth had a cruel thin line to it.

Ira Flint reined in alongside the buggy, his yellowish eyes raking her insolently, undressing her, so that instinctively she shrank

127

back, lifting her hand to pull her coat up tighter over her bosom. She flushed angrily.

"She's come to visit," Wally said, still grinning.

Aline picked up the reins. She felt a nameless terror mount in her.

"I won't bother. I didn't know the Dodds had company." She tried to keep her voice casual. "I'll come by some other time."

"Why it's no bother at all," Flint said, spurring close. "Theresa will be glad to see you. We all will." He grinned. "I'm Theresa's cousin."

Aline picked up the slack in her reins. "I really shouldn't be intruding. I'll come back again," she insisted.

Flint reached down and caught her arm. His voice changed, became hard and cold. "I don't know who you are. But you came to visit. I reckon you'll have to stay!"

Travis edged his mount up close. "That's the girl Ben Codine rode into town with. The one I told you about, Ira."

Aline's eyes went to this man, silently asking for help. "You must be the man who rode out of town with Ben," she said. "Where is he?"

"Ben! So it's Ben to you?" Flint's eyes thinned with understanding. He looked at Travis. "This makes it all the better."

Aline couldn't keep the terror from her voice. "Where is he?" she repeated. And as

Ira swung back to face her: "Who are you?"

Ira's smile held the naked cruelty of a prowling tiger. "We're friends of Ben's. And you'll get to see him tomorrow!"

Travis ignored Aline. "I'll be getting back to town," he told Ira. He swung his cayuse away.

Ira made a motion to Wally who stepped up to the buggy. "I reckon you'd better come inside," he said. "Whether you want to or not, you're staying!"

XI

Fourteen miles southwest of the JD, Conner Creek's ice-rimmed banks sparkled in the bright sunshine filtering through the leafless branches of the cottonwoods. The stream gurgled softly over small twig dams, past the shack that Ira Flint had known as a boy and had remembered as a man fleeing the law.

Slowly the day wore on. Inside the shack the candle in the tin holder on the table flickered in the cold drafts that came through the chinks in the wall. The sacking covering the broken panes in the rear window made little sucking sounds, and this small disturbance only added to the grim silence in the cabin.

Monk had a fire going in the rusted stove. The blaze showed through cracks in the cast iron, making a weaving pattern on the hardpacked, earth floor.

It was still daylight outside, fading into cold twilight, but it began to get gloomy inside the shack. The lone window provided little light. What little there was came from the candle which cast a small circle of shifting illumination over the narrow, home-made bench table and over Ben Codine's tight, hard face.

The bounty hunter was sitting in the only chair with a back; his hands were tied to the sides. His feet were tied, too, but not to the chair.

It was a rickety chair, but it served its purpose. Ben had tried desperately, in the short intervals Monk had stepped outside to gather wood, to work free. But so far he had worked up a sweat, and nothing else.

A rickety cot stood along the side wall, about six feet from where Ben was sitting. Monk had carelessly tossed Ben's gunbelt on that cot when he had come inside the last time. He had his own gun snugged around his paunchy waist; he felt secure enough in his own capabilities to stop Ben without the need of being overly cautious.

The outlaw kept looking at Ben, sneering, as he killed time with a grimy pack of cards. Once in a while he'd lift a hand up to the welt on his jaw, all but obscured by the dark beard stubble.

Daylight faded from the dirty panes. The night seemed to bring a restlessness to Monk, as though some inner doubt was nagging at him.

"So you're the big he-wolf who makes big tracks in Texas!" he snarled abruptly, lifting his eyes to Ben. "Big hombre?" He measured the bounty hunter with a sneer. "But a li'll on the lean side, eh?"

He worked his chaw of tobacco into one cheek and spat his contempt on the floor. "Fast with a gun, mebbe. You'd have to be to'uv killed the Kid. But I'd lay odds I could break you in two with my bare hands!"

It was half a challenge, and Ben's eyes met Monk's, a sudden cold glint in their gray depths.

"Sure, and you've got a big mouth," Codine said bleakly. "I'm figuring it doesn't run as big as your talk, though."

Monk half started up from his chair. Then he sank back, slowly, his eyes narrowing. "No, you don't! I could kill you right here, but Ira wants you kept alive. Until tomorrer."

Ben's laughter was deliberately contemptuous. "You only look big, feller. But most of it's just suet!"

Monk's thick fingers crumpled cards between them. "Suet! I'm from Mississippi, mister. We eat Texans for breakfast." He curled his right arm, bunching a huge bicep. "I was weaned on river boats. I was poling with the best of them before I was sixteen." His laughter jarred mockingly. "Heck, Codine, I said I could break you in two; I don't have to prove it!"

Ben's thoughts worked swiftly. He could not get prodded into a hand-to-hand contest, where the odds at least would be even. But there was another way — a long chance.

"We've got ways in Texas of proving how strong a man is," Ben sneered. "It's an old Indian trick. Apache. Hand to hand on the table."

Monk's eyes glittered. "I've got the stron-gest right arm along the river," he boasted. "It won't be even a close contest."

Ben's eyes surveyed the big man with thin insolence. "It takes more than talk to test a man's strength," he said. He saw Monk waver and he pressed his point. "What have you got to lose? You've got a Colt; mine is over there. All you have to do is free my right hand. You could kill me easy if I tried to make a break."

Monk stood up, peeled off his coat. "You just talked yourself into it. I'll skin yore knuckles so hard you'll have to pry them off the table!"

He walked behind Ben, untied the bounty hunter's right hand. He checked the knots holding his left hand and was satisfied. The tall man's legs were securely tied.

He walked around the table, pushed the candle to the edge, away from them. Sitting, he faced the bounty hunter, the biceps of his thick right arm making a hard knot as he placed his elbow in front of Ben.

The candlelight glinted in his sneering gaze. "We'll see just how big yore mouth is, Codine."

Ben shifted his feet under him, planting them squarely. From here on in his chance to live would depend on split timing, but it was the only chance he'd have.

He propped his right elbow on the table

top and Monk clasped his hand in his huge palm. The burly man's lips twisted in confident leer.

"Ready?" he rasped, and at Ben's nod, Monk's shoulder muscles bunched and the biceps of his right arm made a long hard ridge. He felt the resistance in Ben's hand, solid and rock-like, and surprise rocked through him and thinned his lips. Sweat came out on his forehead as he stared into Ben's smiling face. His neck tendons swelled, a thin sigh escaped from his parted lips.

He couldn't move Ben's arm. Little by little his own was giving ground. A snarl of disbelief died on his lips. He shifted his feet, breaking the rules, and thrust the last spurt of his bull-like strength behind his rigid arm.

The pressure of Ben's hand relented. Monk's hand came up over the starting point and started down, and relief flooded his eyes. He jammed down harshly and the bounty hunter's arm gave way abruptly. His knuckles rapped down in defeat.

Monk settled back in his chair, breathing heavily. "No stayin' power," he sneered.

The sneer was smeared across his lips as Ben's right hand came up and smashed solidly against his mouth. It spun Monk sideways off the seat, sending him sprawling at the foot of the stove.

Ben heaved the bench table over, spinning it out of his way and onto Monk. The man had an iron jaw. He was on his side, shaking his head, a dark bulk revealed only by the flamelight spilling through the stove cracks. The candle had gone out as Ben overturned the table.

The bounty hunter stood up with the chair lashed to his left arm. He flexed his bound legs and jumped in the direction of the cot. The chair hampered him. He tripped and fell and his outstretched right hand hit the edge of the bunk. He clawed for his belt and found it just as Monk shoved the table away from him and lurched up to his feet.

A desperate eternity seemed to pass before Ben's fingers found the smooth butt of his Colt and yanked it free. He was on his elbow, caught in one long flicker of light from the stove. He saw Monk's gun barrel glint in the uncertain light.

The gunflare lighted up Monk's burly figure and Ben fired twice. Monk stumbled and fired once more, his shot wild. Then he took a step toward Ben, and his last word was a curse.

It took Ben a few moments to find the knife on Monk's body. He cut himself free and stood up, lingering only long enough to buckle his gunbelt about his flat waist and find his hat.

His horse, Nig, was tied behind the shack. Flint had brought Monk's horse from the hollow across the creek, where his and

135

Monk's animals had been concealed. Ben had heard that much in the scant conversation that had followed his capture.

Ira had had enough of the big black stallion. Besides, he had answered Travis' query with "it'll look better if they find Codine with the black stud."

Ben stared into the darkness. Somewhere in these hills Flint was hiding out. But he could well spend all night trying to locate the man, tracking him.

There was a better way — a faster way!

He turned Nig toward Labelle.

Paul Shaney watched Travis Paine light his cigar and settle back in his chair. They were both in Paul's hotel room. The sounds of merriment drifted up to them from the lobby. The New Year's Eve celebration was already well under way.

Outside some exuberant puncher let go with his six-gun aimed at the stars; Shaney thought of Mido Peters. The deputy sheriff would have his hands full tonight, even with the two special officers the commissioners had authorized to help him out. Shaney thought of this and relaxed a little, but Travis' news still laid its unsettling hand over him.

This holdup had been his brainchild. He had needed Ira Flint, but he had not reckoned with Ben Codine.

He said worriedly: "Damn it, Travis, why didn't Ira kill that meddling bounty hunter? What's he taking another chance for?"

Travis' dark face remained remote. The man always seemed preoccupied, caught with his own dark thoughts. Finally he shrugged. "Reckon Ira is a gambler, the kind who don't like a sure thing. Besides, I told you what he got planned."

Shaney made a disparaging sound and Travis eyed him coldly. "You gambled yourself, last night, from what I heard." Paul looked at him, lips twisting bitterly.

"Ben Codine is the one man who can spoil everything," he said harshly. "I'm not like Ira. I don't gamble. Not on this thing I worked on for a whole year!"

Shaney walked to the window, peered through the frosted glass, looking down on the street immediately below where the hotel flares cast their flickering shadows. Further up and across the street the Silver Queen was going full blast. He turned slowly and eyed Travis.

"I missed Codine last night. I sure hope Ira doesn't make a mistake with him now."

Travis shrugged. He was a cold man, turned inward. His tomorrows held no futures and he cared little about what could happen. He said coldly: "All we can do is wait, Paul."

Shaney nodded bitterly, turned back to the window. Unlike Travis, his tomorrows meant everything to him.

"Sure," he said thinly, not turning his head. "You and I stay here. When the train doesn't pull in on time, we get up a posse of drunken miners and head them out to the Lucky Try cutoff. We'll find Ben Codine there . . . maybe. We'll find him with a bullet through both legs and an empty satchel in his possession and you and I do a bit of quick talking. And if we talk convincingly enough, we'll have that bounty hunter strung up before the fools start thinking about the empty satchel and where the rest of the holdup men have gone." He paused, half out of breath, his face flushed.

"There's too many maybes, Travis. Maybe we don't find Codine like we're supposed to. Maybe the Special is delayed for other reasons. Maybe the posse won't string him up. Don't forget, Mido Peters will be with us. He isn't a fool."

Travis blew smoke in the bookkeeper's direction. "The maybes are part of the risks," he said coldly.

"To hell with the risks!" Shaney snapped. "There don't have to be risks! At least," he amended harshly, "we don't have to add to them. I've heard of that bounty hunter. Even if only half the stories are true, he's too dangerous a man to monkey with!"

"Monk can handle him," Travis stated calmly. "Codine will be there, in the morning, for us to find." He got up and reached for his hat lying on the small table.

"I'm going out to join the fun at the Grady House. You coming?"

"Later . . . maybe." Shaney's voice was sullen.

Travis' eyes held a touch of contempt. "Sitting here won't change the risks," he pointed out. And added with deep-seated fatalism, "You can play only with the cards you draw in this life."

Shaney stood by the window after Travis had gone. The uneasiness persisted, spreading its dampening aura over his anticipation.

He was through here in Labelle. He had been through from the day Jake Grady had made a surprise audit of his books and found Paul seven thousand dollars short.

A drop in the bucket to the illiterate mick, Shaney thought bitterly. The man had money to throw away, like the thousand-dollar bills he planned to give away tomorrow.

Each man views a problem from his own angle of vision; Shaney eyed his with the bitter logic of a man who thinks himself wronged. That Jake could have sent him to jail for misappropriation of company funds did not come into his consideration. And with his perverse viewpoint he even hated Grady for his leniency.

"I guess a man your age has to hell around some," Grady had said. "Wimmen an' cards an' likker. I ain't condemnin' yuh for that, Paul. But I can't abide a man I can't trust."

Grady had shaken his head. "You could have asked for more money, you know. You've been with me a long time. You could have asked."

He had not turned Shaney over to Mido Peters, nor had he fired him. "It's comin' Christmas time," he had muttered. "I ain't got the heart to fire yuh now. But come the turn of the year, yuh better find yourself another job."

Five years, Shaney recalled sourly, five years he had worked for the Shamrock. For what? For a new thousand-dollar bill handed out to him by a dumb mick who had stumbled upon a fortune and didn't know how to use it?

One hundred and fifty-five thousand dollars split six, no! five ways, now that the Kansas Kid was dead. That meant over thirty-one thousand dollars for him. He could live high in Mexico on that money, or maybe in South America. . . .

He was staring through the panes, occupied with his brooding thoughts, when he saw the rider bulk out of the shadows and move into the firelight toward the hotel hitchrack. It took a moment for Shaney's attention to concentrate on the man. The black sheen of the rider's horse gripped him first. Then the man's face came into the light and an icy hand seemed to close around Shaney's heart, shortening his breath.

"Ben Codine!"

A thousand wild speculations exploded inside his head, only one kept its place. *Flint was a fool!* He'd gambled once before with this bounty hunter. Now he had gambled again. And lost both times!

The risks of the game, Paine had said. A curse welled to his lips. It had always been Ira's outstanding fault, his insufferable need of the dramatic, of being the center of things. Even as a kid Ira was not content to play a game unless he made it dangerous.

This time it could kill him!

Paul stood undecided, not knowing whether to remain in his room, or pack up and leave without a cent just to get out of Labelle while he still had the chance.

Reason laid a calming hand over his rising panic. "You fool!" it whispered. "Codine doesn't know of your part in this. Even if he suspects, he can't prove anything. He's after Ira, anyway, not you. And the fact that he's come to town proves he doesn't know where to find Ira Flint. He's in town looking for Travis."

Shaney walked to the door, opened it. The buzz of voices and the clink of glasses came louder.

Emboldened, he walked to the head of the stairs and stepped down, coming to a stop in the shadows of the mid-landing. He could look down into the lobby now. He saw Codine at the desk, but the clamor from the assemblage by the punch bowl drowned out

Ben's words. He saw the clerk shrug, then one of the men standing by turned and said loudly: "Yeah, I saw the Marshal, fella. I think he was headed for the big shindig up at the Grady House."

Paul saw Ben nod and turn away, and something in the way he walked told him he had not guessed wrong about Codine coming to town for Travis.

He started down to the lobby, an idea running through the panic in him, shaping finally into decisive action. He had to see Mido Peters. He had to find the deputy sheriff before it was too late.

XII

Ben Codine turned Nig away from the hotel
rack and headed up the street toward the
Grady house. He threaded his way past several
light wagons and gigs heading in the same
direction. A half-dozen riders swept up and
clattered past him, eager to get to the Grady
shindig.

The bounty hunter kept his deadly urgency
under control. He would have to find his
man in that crowd of merrymakers and take
him alive. He would not make the mistake he
had with the Kansas Kid; he had to get
Travis alive and make him talk.

The Grady house loomed up on the slope,
a mile from town. Its lower levels were ablaze
with light and he heard the noise of laughter
and the tin clatter of merrymakers long before
he turned into the big yard area in front of
the building.

The gray stone monstrosity, bleak and in-
hospitable for much of the year, was warmed
tonight by a milling throng which spilled out
along the wide stone veranda. The front por-
tals were illuminated by wrought-iron, brack-
eted oil lamps.

Codine ground-reined the black stallion between two gigs and pushed through the crowd

in the hallway and turned to the blare of music coming through an archway on his right.

This opened to the Grady ballroom, a huge room brilliantly lighted by a dozen crystal chandeliers.

Codine's gaze roamed over the dancers, moving to a Virginia reel. He found the man he wanted across the room, standing by a long table loaded with food and tended by servants in white jackets.

Travis was talking to a red-faced, smiling man in a cutaway Prince Albert coat. The man looked about as much at home in those clothes as a shaggy-haired mule on a Kentucky race track.

Ben had the feeling he was looking at Jake Grady. There was something amiable and shy in that creased face, and he was smiling with the happy expression of a man who liked to see others have fun.

Ben edged his way through the crowd. Few people paid any attention to him. The Grady shindigs were wide open to any who cared to attend.

The music ended and the dancers broke up, most of the men heading for the bar in the other room. Several children started to skate across the slicked-down oak floor.

Travis caught a glimpse of Ben Codine coming up. He turned quickly, surprise smearing the smile from his eyes. Codine's

Colt muzzled him, halting his instinctive motion toward the holster gun partially hidden by his coat.

Only Travis and Grady seemed to be aware of Ben's presence, of the gun in Ben's hand. Grady said sharply: "Just a minnit, feller. What's the meaning of this?"

Ben's hard tone silenced him. "The Marshal and I have business, Mr. Grady. Keep your mouth shut, or a lot of innocent people will likely get hurt!"

Grady glanced at the laughing, milling throng. He nodded, his face almost childlike in its wondering stillness.

A stiff smile cracked Travis Paine's lips. "Business, hell!" he muttered.

Ben's voice was grim as death. "We're stepping outside, Marshal!" He stressed the word *marshal*. "We've got a little call to make. Only this time we'll find the man I'm after."

"Go to the devil!" Travis said. He said it distinctly, and several men turned their heads, and Ben knew then that this man, too, like the Kansas Kid, would be hard to handle. A savage bitterness crowded into his voice.

"That's just where you're headed!" he muttered, stepping close. "After you lead me to Ira Flint!"

He saw Travis' gaze flick to something behind him, and the flicker in those dark pupils warned him even before he heard the flat sound of boots on the dance floor behind him.

Then Mido Peters' harsh voice cut through that stilling murmur of voice:

"Drop that gun, Codine, or I'll collect that reward for your hide, anyway! With your dead body!"

There was a finality in the deputy sheriff's tone that held the bounty hunter from the savage impulse to whirl and make a break. He turned slowly, his gun lowering to his side, a bitter frustration riding him, turning him sour. He had not counted on Peters being here.

He faced the deputy sheriff who was standing flat-footed a dozen feet away. One of Mido's special deputies stood beside him, a gun in his hand, a cold sweat on his face.

Then Ben saw Paul Shaney hanging back in the crowd by the archway, and he made that connection now between Jake Grady's bookkeeper and the phony U.S. Marshal. And he understood how Peters came to be here so opportunely.

He saw this, and then Travis made his move. The outlaw's hand swept up from under his coat; and it was this blur of movement that Ben caught out of his eye corners.

Travis was remembering the Kansas Kid. He fired before his muzzle was level and the slug missed Ben's whirling body and ripped through the leg of a miner across the hall.

His second shot splintered the floor in front of him as he buckled to the hot lead in his chest. Travis fell slowly, trying to stand, but not making it.

Ben's shots had been instinctive, knowing he had no choice. The split-second action caught Mido and his deputy by surprise; by the time they cocked trigger they were staring into Ben's leveled Colt.

The sweat glistened on Peters' forehead. "You'll have to get us both!" he grated. "And even then you'll never make it out that door, Codine!"

Ben nodded, the harsh look in his eyes fading. "I want no trouble with you, Peters, nor do I want a lot of innocent people hurt." He lowered his gun arm and skidded his Colt toward the lawman.

The look on Mido Peters' hard face changed slightly, but his voice held a thin edge of suspicion. "I don't know why you gunned him," he nodded to the man on the floor, "but I'll see that you hang for it, Codine!"

Ben made a short motion with his empty hands. "Hear me out first, Peters. I am Ben Codine."

"The bounty hunter turned outlaw!" Peters cut in harshly. "I'll hear you out, all right — behind cell bars!"

There was no arguing with the man now, Ben saw. He turned to Travis. The outlaw's eyes were open; he was still alive. Ben knelt beside him, ignoring the sharp warning in Mido's voice.

"Where's Flint hiding out?" he asked grimly. He voiced the question, knowing it was his last chance to find out, and knowing that even if this man talked, it might not help him now.

Travis' pupils burned with bitter hatred. "You . . . go . . . to hell!"

Then Peters' hard hand was on Ben Codine's shoulder, pulling him back.

Codine said desperately, turning: "Hear me out, Peters! This man is no United States Marshal. He's one of the Ira Flint gang, the outlaw who's been posing as Ben Codine."

He saw the sneer on Peters' lips and he sensed that no amount of talk would convince this lawman.

He took the risk of his move being misinterpreted and reached inside his boot for the letter from his brother-in-law. It was his last resort.

"Read it!" he said harshly. "It's a letter from Sheriff Tolliver; it'll prove who I am."

Peters thrust the envelope into his pocket. "Later," he said grimly. "After I have you behind bars!"

The bounty hunter paced the narrow confines of his cell while outside in his office Mido Peters read Sheriff Bill Tolliver's letter with cynical disbelief.

The letter bore the heading of the county sheriff's office, Nueces County, Texas, and it was signed by Bill Tolliver. The sheriff's name meant nothing to Mido Peters. The letter was short and crisp:

To Whomever It May Concern:
The man who has this letter is Ben Codine. He is my brother-in-law. I put my oath to this testimony. The man who has been posing as Ben Codine is Ira Flint, a killer wanted by the State of Texas, a man already sentenced to hang for past crimes. I swear that this is true. If the bearer of this letter needs help, give it to him. If you need further proof, wire me.

Peters crumpled the letter in his fist and tossed it on his desk. Ron Sawyer, one of his special officers, a younger man, picked it up. He read it while Peters paced the floor.

"Cripes!" Ron muttered. He looked at the deputy sheriff. "What if this is on the level, Peters?"

Mido sneered. But his own small doubt was strengthened by Ron's tone.

"If this was written by that Nueces County sheriff, then the rest of Codine's story makes sense, Peters," the younger man persisted. "He told us he was shot by one of Ira Flint's men while he was taking that outlaw to King City. Flint took his horse, his papers, even

149

his gun. It could just be like he says."

Peters stopped by the desk and looked down at the letter. "It rings true all right!" he snapped, "until you look close at it, Ron. What darned fool would leave a man as dangerous as that bounty hunter alive when another shot would have finished him? Why would any man risk masquerading as Ben Codine? And why . . . ?" he gritted his teeth, "why did Flint come here to Labelle? Where is this killer who looks enough like the real Ben Codine to pass himself off as that Texas bounty hunter?"

Ron lifted his shoulder. "I don't know. But that doesn't make it impossible." He glanced at the letter. "Why don't we send a wire to that Texas sheriff, like it says? If he can describe the man we've got in our jail, even to the scar still puckering his chest, if he can send us a personal question to ask Ben Codine, that ought to be proof enough, Peters."

Peters weighed this stubborn logic against his growing indecision. The story Ben Codine had told him did ring true. He had come to Labelle after the outlaw who had taken his identity and his horse; he had found the big black stallion running free on the edge of town. That part of Ben's story checked; Mido had verified it with Rio Vegas —

The deputy sheriff was interrupted by the arrival of his other special officer, Hank Lentz, an older, no-nonsense man. Hank glanced at Peters and Ron and shrugged.

"That Marshal feller just died," he announced grimly. "He never regained consciousness."

Ron was silent, staring at Peters. The deputy sheriff turned, put his hard gaze on the closed cell block door. Even this part of Ben's story would take time to check out. A wire to the District U.S. Marshal's office to check the number of Travis Paine's badge against the man who had worn it would take a day or two at least. Peters sighed bitterly. And time was what he didn't have . . . not now, not this New Year's Eve.

Somewhere out in the night a special train out of Denver was speeding toward Labelle carrying one hundred and fifty-five thousand dollars.

He turned back to Hank, his lips tightening harshly. "You've lived in this part of the country longer than either of us, Hank," he said. "You ever hear of a man named Ira Flint?"

Hank frowned. "Ira . . . Ira . . . ?" He knuckled the stubble on his jaw. "Yeah . . . useta be a kid with that name . . . lived with the Dodds." He eyed Peters curiously. "I think he was a nephew of Jesse Dodd's."

"Ever hear from him or about him?" Peters muttered.

Hank shook his head. "Always figgered he'd wind up behind bars." As Peters and Ron looked closely at him: "He was a pretty wild kid when I knew him. Never gave Jesse anything but trouble. He finally ran away . . .

151

about fifteen or sixteen years ago . . ."

Peters sucked in a troubled breath. "You're sure about this, Hank?"

Hank nodded. "My folks owned a small farm a few miles east of the Dodds. I went over there a few times. Jesse was a hardworking man, but Ira . . ." Hank paused and frowned. "Why all the questions about him, Peters?"

Peters indicated the letter on his desk. Hank picked it up and read it. He nodded to himself once or twice, then turned to look at Peters.

"It makes sense," he said slowly. "In a crazy way, it would be just the kind of thing Ira Flint would pull."

Peters made a fist of his right hand, punched it into the palm of his left in frustrated anger. "All right, if Ira Flint did come back to Labelle, where would he hide out? And why?"

Hank shrugged. "He could be staying at his uncle's place. It's far enough from town, and pretty isolated from the main roads. Why he came . . . ?" Hank looked closely at Peters, his voice falling off: "He couldn't have known about the money, could he?"

Peters made an angry gesture and walked to the window. "I don't know anything any more, Hank." He stared out into the street, not seeing anything. He was going over the thorny possibilities opened up by Hank's revelation.

"It's a hell of a ride out to Jesse's place, just to find out. . . ." His muttered words dropped off as he turned slowly to face Hank. He couldn't *ask* this man to ride out there.

Hank said quietly: "It's worth a check, Peters." He smiled. "I haven't seen old Jesse in almost a year. I owe him a New Year's greeting."

Ron said: "I'll ride with you."

Hank shook his head. "If Ira's there, two of us showing up will mean trouble."

Peters indicated the badge on Hank's coat. "Better leave that behind," he suggested.

Hank nodded. He unpinned his star, dropped it into a desk drawer. He slid his Colt out of holster, checked it carefully, then slid it back. He blew gently on his hands.

Peters shook his head. "Hank, the more I think about it the more I don't like it. If Ira Flint is holed up at the Dodd place. . . ."

"That's what we want to know, isn't it?" Hank cut in quietly. He shrugged. "Ira couldn't know I'm working for the law. I'm just a neighbor, dropping by to say hello to Jesse."

He turned to the cell block door, his thoughts on Ben Codine. "You know, Mido," he added thoughtfully, "he could be right. Ira's hair was light, but if he darkened it . . . ?"

"According to that Texas sheriff, Ira's due to hang," Ron muttered. "He'll be as dangerous as a treed panther."

Hank walked to the door. Peters headed

him off and they looked at each other for a brief moment, then Peters stuck out his hand. Hank took it, self-consciously.

"I'll be back by morning," Hank said.

Peters nodded. "We'll be waiting."

Hank went out, closing the door behind him. Peters looked at Ron, his teeth grating edgily. "Five dollars a day ain't enough pay for what he's doing!"

Outside a couple of wild shots stabbed into the cold night. But Mido Peters ignored them. He was no longer concerned with drunks and Jake Grady's holiday shindig. He made a gesture to the cell door.

"Let's go back and have a talk with Ben Codine!"

The bounty hunter came off his bunk as Peters and his special deputy came down the short cell block corridor. Ben's eyes measured the sober faces of the lawmen.

"Travis is dead," Peters said bluntly. "He died without talking."

Codine let out his breath in a disappointed sigh. "He was my last hope," he said grimly. Then his eyes narrowed as a new thought hit him. "That Grady bookkeeper, Shaney, I saw him with Travis a few times." As Peters frowned: "You said he vouched for Travis. Where is he?"

Peters shook his head. "What has Paul Shaney got to do with this?"

"I don't know," Ben admitted. "But Shaney

was very friendly with Travis, and I know Travis was no U.S. Marshal. I told you about his leading me into a trap at that shack on Conner Creek."

"You told me a lot of things," Peters growled. "If Ira Flint *is* around, what's he up to? What's he waiting for?"

Ben shook his head. "All I know he's got something planned for tomorrow."

Peters glanced worriedly at Ron Sawyer. He was sharply aware now of the money coming in from Denver. If Ira knew about Grady's New Year's handout, it would explain his coming here. And if Paul Shaney was mixed up in this . . . ?

He took a long breath. "I reckon I'm being a damn fool," he told Ben. "But I'm going to send that wire to Sheriff Tolliver."

He turned to Ron Sawyer. "And let's have a talk with Paul Shaney."

XIII

Only Rio Vegas noticed Paul Shaney leave town. Vegas was aware of this because Shaney came to see him about borrowing the blue roan the livery man had for hire. He told Vegas he would be back before morning and Vegas accepted this, knowing no reason why Shaney should not be back.

Paul was not a good rider, but he kept the stable-rested animal to a hard run. It was eleven o'clock when he slid out of saddle, stiff and saddle-sore, and stumbled toward the darkened JD ranchhouse.

A figure appeared in the shadow of the barn door. Wally Mathis was sleeping light tonight. His voice cut across the yard, pulling Shaney around.

"Ira! I've got to see Ira! I'm Paul Shaney!"

His voice rode high through the cold stillness. Wally came toward him, moving deliberately, his rifle held ready.

No light appeared against the ranchhouse windows, but the door opened and Flint's tall figure bulked in the opening. His voice had a sleepy growl: "What in hell brings you out here, Paul?"

"*Codine!*" Fear rode nakedly across Shaney's high-pitched voice. "He just killed

Travis! He's in Labelle."

"Codine!" Ira's roused tone cut harshly at the frightened man. "You're shying at shadows, you damn fool! Ben Codine's in a shack south of here, tied hand and foot. He can't be —"

"He's in Labelle!" Shaney snarled, desperation making him defiant of this man. "You're the damn fool, Ira! You should have killed him when you had the chance."

Wally's voice came between them, strangely calm in this moment. "If Codine's in town it means Monk is dead. He's in town lookin' for you, Ira, or he would have been here by now." He shot a look at Shaney. "Unless Travis told him?"

Shaney shook his head. "Travis kept his mouth shut." A measure of control came to him with Wally's calmness. "He's in jail right now. Peters took him in. He's holding him until he gets some kind of verification from a Sheriff Tolliver in Nueces County, Texas. I didn't hang around to find out what kind."

Flint began to chuckle. "He killed Monk; he must have. And he's gunned down Travis. I underestimated him, Wally," he admitted. "But he's in a cell right now, wondering where I am! Wondering what I'm up to!" The old cruel insolence laughed in his voice. "Let him sweat! We'll pull that raid in the morning and be a long way from here before he gets out. *If* he does get out!"

Wally cut in curtly. "When we started out there were five of us. Not counting . . ." He glanced at Shaney. "Now there's only you and me."

"Paul's here!" Flint said grimly, "and my ace in the hole!" He turned and stared with slitted gaze into the darkness of the ranchhouse. "Our ace in the hole, Wally."

Mido Peters found the night telegrapher in the Silver Queen, sobered him up enough to sit him at the key and spelled out his message to Sheriff Tolliver. He made the man promise to stand by the wire until he received a reply, then he and Ron Sawyer went out to find Paul Shaney.

Paul was not at his hotel nor was he at the Grady shindig which had continued, somewhat subdued, after the shooting of Travis Paine. Grady's bookkeeper, Peters reflected, could be anywhere. But a gnawing discontent began to worry the deputy sheriff.

They were coming back along Lodestone Avenue when Peters saw someone go into his office. He had hired no one to stand by as jailer, figuring that most of the night's offenders would be drunks and only too glad to sleep it off in one of his cells. He had forgotten that a man like Ben Codine might have friends ready to risk a jail break. . . .

He and Ron cut across the street for the office at a run, came up on the walk and by the lone window overlooking the street. Peters suddenly put a hand out to Ron's arm, checking the deputy's move toward his gun.

"It's Mrs. Buskin," he said quietly. He could see her through the window, standing helplessly by his desk. "Check with Rio," he ordered Sawyer. "Find out if Shaney hired one of his animals to leave town. I'll see what Mrs. Buskin wants."

Mary Buskin was on her way out when Mido entered. She was glad to see him.

"I hoped to find you here," she said. She looked tired, worried. "Such a wild crowd out there."

He nodded gravely. "How's Tommy?"

"He's fine," she said automatically. Obviously Tommy was not her concern at this moment. "It's Aline. She hasn't come home."

Peters frowned, hiding the sharp prod of intuition that gripped him.

"Where'ud she go, Mary?" He knew the Buskins well enough for this sort of familiarity; he had been invited to supper quite a few times. He liked Harvey and he liked Aline, but it had never progressed to anything more than that. He had his own reservations concerning himself, where Aline was concerned, and Aline had shown that her friendliness was nothing more than that.

Mary sighed. "She went out to visit Theresa Dodd. She promised me she'd be back before night."

"The Dodds?" The question was sharp, involuntary, and Mary eyed him closely, worried by something she sensed in Peters' tone. "Why . . . is there something wrong out there?"

Peters hesitated, then: "I don't know," he said quietly. "Hank has gone to find out."

Mary clutched at his arm, her anxiety not eased by his reply.

"What is it?" she demanded. "What could possibly have happened to the Dodds?"

"Probably nothing," Peters said quietly. Then, knowing she wouldn't go without some sort of explanation he added: "There's been rumors of an outlaw, out of Texas, heading this way. He may have tried to hide out at the Dodd place. It's somewhat out of the way —"

Mary's fingers tightened on his arm. "Aline!" she cried. "Something must have happened!"

"Hank's on his way there now," Peters said sharply. "I don't think there's anything to the rumor, but Hank will find out." He glanced back to the open door where shouts of half drunken miners, staggering down the street toward the Silver Queen attracted his attention.

"You shouldn't be out on the streets alone, Mary," he said gently. "Where's Harvey?"

"He's not at home," she said bitterly, "or he would have gone to the Dodd place himself. He's sleeping at the shack up at the spur tonight."

"Well, go on home," Peter said gently.

160

"There's nothing you can do here. And Aline may have been invited to spend the night with Theresa." He smiled. "You know how little company they have."

Mary nodded. It wasn't the first time Aline had done just that. But Aline had promised to come back home tonight.

Peters sensed her hesitation. "Hank will be back in the morning, Mary. Aline will probably be riding with him." He turned her to the door. "Want me to walk you home?"

She shook her head. "I'll manage . . . it's not far."

Peters watched her leave. Behind him an old wall clock ticked softly, undeterred by human events. It was almost midnight. Soon bedlam would break loose in Labelle as several thousand people, miners, farmers, townspeople and the Lord knew who else, and in what stage of inebriation, greeted the New Year.

He wondered bleakly what Hank Lentz would find at the Dodd ranch.

He turned to the cell block, looked in at Ben Codine. Ben was at the window, looking out. There was little he could see from there except a small patch of night sky, the narrow confines of an alley. Ben turned as Peters opened the cell block door. Peters just stood there, eyeing him, not saying anything. After a few moments he closed the door and turned back to his desk . . .

Ron Sawyer came in a few minutes later.

He had news of Paul Shaney.

"Shaney left town right after we jailed Codine," he said. There was a fever of excitement in his voice. "On New Year's Eve Paul Shaney hired Vegas' big blue roan and goes out for a ride." He moved up to Peters, his eyes glinting. "It checks out, Peters." As Mido didn't say anything. "Let me ride out after Hank?"

Peters shook his head. "We'll wait." Ron's face registered a sharp disappointment. "I need you here," Peters added. He made a gesture toward the door. "It could all be a trick," he added tightly, "a trick to get us out of town. Leave it wide open for Ira, or. . . ." He turned to look back toward the cell block. "I'm still not sure about Ben Codine. And until I am, we'll wait here!"

Aline Buskin huddled in a chair in Theresa's room, sleepless, gripped by a growing terror. Theresa, her fever rising during the night, had slept fitfully. She was sleeping now, a restless, uneasy sleep. She stirred and moaned softly and then, turning, she woke with a start and started to sit up.

Martha Dodd rose immediately from her position by the door and came to her daughter's bedside where Aline joined her. Both women were shadowy figures. The light on the dresser behind them was turned down and the shade in the lone window pulled all the way down.

Theresa's eyes had a too bright look. They

searched Aline's face for a moment, then clung to her mother's.

"Have they gone?" she whispered.

Martha shook her head. She had been sleepless for the past two nights, standing guard at her daughter's door. Her face was worn, tired.

"They're leaving in the morning," she said. "Try to sleep."

Theresa's eyes went to Aline . . . her hand reached out, trembling, for Aline's hand. She looked at her mother. "Why do they want to take Aline with them?" she whispered.

Martha Dodd's lips tightened to a thin fine line. "They won't," she said. "Now you just lay back and try to sleep."

Theresa eased slowly back on her pillow. Her eyes closed. She said bitterly, "Why did he have to come back . . . now . . . after all these years?"

Martha Dodd looked at Aline. "You, too," she said softly. "Get some rest —"

She broke off as beyond the bedroom door Wally's voice carried sharply: "Ira . . . there's someone else riding out there tonight!"

Aline Buskin and Martha Dodd exchanged glances.

Inside the Dodd kitchen a match, snapped to small flame, was carried to the oil lamp on the table. It flared to brighter glow as the wick caught. It was turned down immediately, leaving a small circle of illumination that

163

barely encompassed the table on which it sat.

Wally was holding his rifle ready. He was in the shadows by the door and only barely visible. Ira tossed the burnt match aside and stepped away from the table, motioning to Paul Shaney to get out of sight, in Jesse Dodd's room. Then he turned to the door.

Outside the ring of iron-shod hoofs on frozen ground rang clearly. The rider was making no attempt to conceal his approach. Ira eased up beside Wally and waited.

The caller rode up to the door and stopped. Then a voice, slightly thickened, called: "Jesse . . . you old son of a gun! You up?"

Ira looked at Wally, frowning. Some neighbor calling at this hour? Then he grinned coldly. What the hell, it *was* New Year's Eve! He turned quickly and crossed to Jesse's room.

Jesse was sitting on the edge of his bed, drawing on a pair of pants over his longjohns. Ira said in a cold low voice: "See what the fool wants, then send him away!"

Jesse stumbled to his feet, wordless, and went into the kitchen, hitching his galluses over his shoulder. Wally, by the door, shot him a look.

From outside Hank's voice lifted: "Come to see the New Year in with yuh, Jesse. Come on, open up!"

Jesse looked back to Ira who nodded. Jesse crossed to the door and opened it. The light was at his back, outlining him and spilling past him in wan glow to the rider in front of the stairs.

Jesse said: "It's late, Hank. And Theresa's not feeling well."

But Hank was already dismounting. He lurched slightly, as though he had taken a few drinks too early. He came up the stairs to Jesse, a grin on his face and a pint bottle in his hand.

"Brought you a New Year's present, Jesse," he said, holding it out. "Man needs a little relaxation, once a year." He stopped as Jesse barred the way. "Aw, come on, Jesse," he said, "I rode a long way to wish you and the family a happy New Year."

Jesse said: "Thanks, Hank. But Theresa and Martha are asleep."

Hank pushed inside, past him. "They'll be glad to see me, Jesse; they always have." He was close to the table now, in the light. His gaze swung swiftly over the room and he reacted as Wally moved in from the wall by the door, the rifle in his hands held loosely but deceptively dangerous.

"Oh!" Hank said slowly, his gaze going to Jesse. "Sorry . . . I didn't know you had company."

Jesse didn't say anything. Wally studied Hank for a beat; he had never seen the man before. "Where'd you come from . . . town?"

Hank was looking at Jesse, wondering at the man's silence. This small man was not Ira, but he felt certain Ira was in the house somewhere. A small prickle tingled his back.

"No," he replied to Wally. "I live up the valley a piece."

"You're a liar, Hank!" The voice came from behind him small and bitter, and he recognized it, even before he turned. It wasn't Ira's voice!

Paul Shaney moved out of the shadow, toward the table. He stood watching Hank, his eyes bitter, then he turned as Ira moved up beside him.

"Peters must have smelled a rat, Ira! This is Hank Lentz, one of his special deputies!"

Ira looked at Hank across the table. The name was familiar, so was the face. But it was a long way across the years.

"Happy New Year, Hank," he said softly and drew and fired in one swift motion.

Hank was spinning back, trying to reach his gun when the bullets hit him. He staggered across the room and fell at Jesse Dodd's feet. He had managed to get his gun out of holster, but he died without firing it.

Jesse Dodd stared at Ira. "You cold-blooded, senseless murderer!" he choked. "You . . . you. . . ." He dropped to his knees, his fingers clawing for the gun in Hank's hand.

Wally stepped up, clubbed him across the back of the head with the stock of his rifle. Jesse sprawled across Hank's body, unconscious.

Ira came around the table, his gun still

166

cocked in his hand. He stood over Jesse's body, muzzle pointing down at his uncle's head.

"Ira!" Martha's voice was a scream. She lunged out of Theresa's room, crossing to Ira, clawing at his gun hand. He shoved her roughly against the wall.

"I'm not going to kill him," he said coldly. "Just keep the old fool quiet."

He reached down, pulled Jesse away from Hank's body, and motioned to Shaney to give him a hand. Together they carried Jesse into his room, dropped him on his bed.

Coming back into the kitchen Ira looked at Wally. "All right," he decided. "Saddle up! One for the girl. We'll leave the rig. Shoot the animals we leave behind!"

Wally nodded. "Take us a good six hours to get there. Be daylight —"

Shaney cut him off. "The Special's not due at the cutoff until eight." He turned to Ira. "What if we're seen?"

"A chance we'll have to take!" Ira snapped. He motioned to Hank's body. "Give Wally a hand and dump him somewhere out in back of the barn."

He turned, walked to Theresa's bedroom door. Aline was by the bed, near Theresa. He looked at her for a long moment, eyes cruel, laughing. He made a motion, crooking his finger to her.

"Come on, Miss Buskin. We've got a long ride ahead of us!"

XIV

The night dragged into the small hours of morning. A damper had been clamped on the celebration at the Grady house and the party had broken up earlier than had been planned. But late revelers still roamed Labelle's cold streets. A half-dozen times small groups of tipsy miners had come to the law office wanting to get their hands on the "damned killer" who had shot a United States Marshal, only to be turned away by Mido Peters and his special deputy.

A mob could easily have been turned into a lynching party this night, but there was no one in Labelle to give it direction, to fan the incipient spark.

A gray dawn came to run cold fingers along the horizon, lightening Ben Codine's cell. Ben paused in his restless pacing, a gray despair killing his dwindling hopes.

The cell block door opened and Mido Peters came down the corridor. He was holding a telegram in his hand. Ron Sawyer was behind him.

Peters eyed Ben grimly. "I got an answer to my wire," he told Codine. "What's the name of Sheriff Tolliver's wife? Her nickname?"

"My sister? Kit." The name leaped to

Ben's lips unthinkingly. He saw Peters' eyes narrow. He glanced at his deputy and nodded.

Ron came up to Ben's cell door and unlocked it.

"Reckon I've been a fool, Codine," Peters said. "This wire proves it. Sheriff Tolliver's description tallies, even to that small scar under your chin. And no one but you would have known the name of Sheriff Tolliver's wife."

Ben pushed past Peters, into the office. "There's no time for name calling, Peters," he said curtly. "Maybe there's no time left at all." He was buckling his gun belt around his waist. "Have you found Paul Shaney?"

Peters shook his head. "Shaney left town last night. He said he'd be back, but he didn't show up. My guess is he joined Ira Flint at the Dodd ranch."

Ben spun around to face Peters. "The Dodd ranch? You knew . . . about Ira?"

Peters' voice was bitter. "No. I began to suspect last night. When Hank told me he had known Ira Flint, that Ira was Jesse Dodd's nephew. I guessed then that if you were right about Ira, and he had come to Labelle, he would be hiding out at his uncle's place." He was silent a moment. "Hank rode out there last night."

Ben's thoughts were racing ahead of Peters, pulling fragments of what he had heard into a pattern. With Shaney definitely linked to Ira Flint, the outlaw's plans had to concern the Shamrock.

He turned to Peters. "What would Grady's bookkeeper know? What would bring Flint back to Labelle?"

Mido Peters' lips twisted harshly. "One hundred and fifty-five thousand dollars! Coming in on the Denver Special . . . due in today . . . this morning." He caught Ben's narrowing look and made a bitter, offhand gesture. "A load I've been carrying on my back for a week, Ben. One hundred and fifty-five crisp new thousand-dollar bills, money Jake Grady planned to hand out as New Year's gifts to his employees."

Ben spun around for the door. This was the last piece to fall into place. It fitted into the groove between Harvey Buskin's quick-caught remark at supper the other night that a special train was coming through the Gap at eight-thirty, and Flint's parting sneer at the Conner Creek shack before he left him with Monk Ulley.

It had to be the Special at the Lucky Try cutoff!

Peters reached the door behind him with his deputy crowding him. "Where are you headed?" he yelled after Ben. He heard the answer, but Mido Peters stood there, not following. His mind worked slower than that of the bounty hunter's. Why at the Lucky Try

170

cutoff? What if Ira Flint was after bigger game? There was close to ten times the amount riding in the Denver Special in Labelle's stone bank!

He was still undecided when Ben Codine rode Nig out of the stable yard and in the gray winter dawn headed for the steel rails bisecting the cold hills.

Full daylight found Harvey Buskin out of the railroad shack and backing his handcar onto the Lucky Try spur, out of the way of the coming train. He had gone out at daybreak to check the tracks through the Gap, looking for fallen rocks, a sprung rail. He had found the line in good condition. Now, with the handcar out of the way, he walked back to throw the switch into place and lock it, and looked toward the Gap again.

A quiet, settled man, Harvey had not regretted missing the wild New Year's Eve celebration in town. He was mildly worried about Tommy, not because of the boy's wound, which was minor, but because of certain wild tendencies cropping up in the boy. And Aline . . . ?

His thoughts swung around to the man called Ben who had come to supper the night before. He had picked up some startling news before coming up here. From Vegas he had heard of the killing of the Kansas Kid in the barn. There were hints that the man who had saved Aline's life was fleeing from the law in Texas.

It was unsettling news, and Harvey tried to sort out these disturbing facts, not being able to make them jibe with the feeling he had of the man who had sat across the table from him. He knew how Aline felt about Ben . . . and true or not, his daughter would be hurt.

He made a last inspection of the track beyond the switch on foot and came back to the shack. He glanced at his pocket watch. He still had a half hour before the Special would sound its warning whistle.

He turned to the shack door and started to fit his key into the padlock. He would throw a little more coal into the stove.

He heard the riders move through the brush behind the shack and he paused, wondering who was about so early. And all at once the slow interest in him blanked out; his face grayed, aged by a score of years. He stood frozen, watching the riders as they pulled up, the foremost so close that the breathing of his horse plumed into his face.

Harvey recognized two of the four. Paul Shaney, sitting tight and nervous on Rio Vegas' blue roan. And his daughter, Aline, slumped forward in saddle, a livid welt on her left cheek, a dazed look in her eyes.

Above him Flint's cruel voice overrode the soft, tired snorting of the horses. "Open up, Pop! You've got company!"

Harvey was too stunned to obey. Flint dismounted, shoved him aside, and opened the door. He grabbed the switchman by the collar and spun him inside. His voice was flat and impatient. "You'll move, by hell, when I tell you to! And you'll do exactly as I say! Or you and this girl of yours will wind up in a gully!"

He turned and pulled Aline down from her saddle and shoved her through the doorway. His voice reached out to Wally, sitting small and silent in saddle.

"You know what to do! We've got less than thirty minutes!"

Wally gathered up the reins of the animals as Shaney dismounted and rode with them into the brush behind the shack. Shaney joined Flint inside the shack.

Flint was talking to Harvey who was standing, dumb, heart-stricken, beside his daughter.

"You're going to stop the Special, Pop. Just ahead of that switchoff. I want the engineer and his fireman to join you on the tracks, and I want that baggage car door opened. I don't care what you tell them: say you have a message from Jake Grady, say anything! *But I want that baggage door opened!*"

Harvey nodded dumbly. He looked at Aline, his eyes asking a thousand silent questions. At Flint's snarled order, he shook down the ashes in the pot-bellied stove, added fresh coal. Ira and Shaney warmed their cold hands over the hot plate. Shaney didn't even react to Harvey's accusing look. He was past all caution now. All he wanted was his split of the money and a chance to make the Mexican border.

Wally didn't join them. But Harvey Buskin didn't even wonder what the small man was up to.

It was eight-twenty-five when the Denver Special sent its warning whistle that it had crested the Gap and would be coming down the long grade to Labelle.

Harvey reached inside the wooden box for the red flares and went out. He walked along the track, knowing only that his daughter was in that shack with a gun leveled at her head. He walked like a dead man, dragging his feet.

The engineer of the Special saw the red flares along the track ahead as he nosed the engine around the jut of rock at the Gap and eased back on the throttle. The flares smoked along the railbed about two miles down. A small figure was standing in the middle of the tracks, waving his arms, and he recognized Harvey Buskin.

He reached up and yanked the cord overhead. The steam blast whipped back over the tender and the baggage car that made up the train. It would cost Jake Gady a pretty penny for this special run, the engineer speculated.

He cut steam altogether and applied the brakes as the red flares loomed up. He could see Harvey's face plainly now. The man looked sick this morning. Hell, he thought sympathetically, the man was getting a little too old for this kind of work.

The engineer ground the big drive wheels to a stop and leaned out of his cab window. "What's wrong, Harvey?"

The switchman waved his arms. "Can't hear you," he yelled above the heavy sighing of the boiler. "Come on down here."

The engineer glanced at his fireman. "Something's wrong, Jack. Never knew Harvey to act like this before."

They swung down the iron ladders and walked up to join Harvey. Jack, a stocky youngster, grinned impudently. "Hell of a way to start the New Year, Harvy."

Buskin glanced back to the shack; his voice was thick with fear as he blurted out: "I've got to see the messenger in the baggage car. I've got a message from Grady for him."

The engineer scratched his head. "We've got orders to keep that door locked, Harv. Until we pull into Labelle and Sheriff Peters takes charge."

"Devil with that, man!" Harvey said desperately. He was thinking of his girl in the shack; she meant more to him than all of Grady's money. "I told you Jake Grady wants me to give him a message."

"All right, Harv," Jack said, putting an arm affectionately over the switchman's shoulder. "We'll get him for you." He turned and walked along the engine to the baggage car and pounded on the door.

"Radisek!" he yelled. "Harvey Buskin wants to talk to you! Message from Jake Grady."

Bolts snicked back. Then the door squealed harshly on its iron track. A heavy Polish face jutted in the opening, scowling down at Jack. "Tell him to come here!" Radisek growled.

Jack turned and waved to Harvey. "Radisek says for you to come —"

His mouth hung open as the baggage messenger above him seemed to come apart, sag in the middle. The rifle crack from the brush behind him seemed oddly disconnected from the happening.

Radisek was falling toward him when the fireman turned. Wally's second bullet hit him in the side, and then the messenger's heavy body fell across him.

The engineer stood frozen for a bleak moment of confusion, then he broke into a run toward the limp figures. He didn't even get to see the man who came out of the switchman's shack and leveled a Colt at him. He felt the smash of the bullet and the roadbed seemed to come up and meet his face, and nothing else mattered.

Flint plunged past Harvey, discounting the small figure. Behind him Shaney was coming out of the shack, a Colt in his hand. He could be counted on to keep Harvey in line.

Ira reached the baggage car just as Wally emerged from the brush, holding his rifle. Flint's voice was quick, approving. "Good work, Wally." He stepped callously on Radisek's body and heaved himself up and into the baggage car.

In the stillness the engine made the only sound, a panting like some patiently waiting animal.

Ben Codine came into sight of the train with the sound of the shots echoing in his ears. He came up in time to see Flint disappear into the baggage car, and to lay his hard glance on Paul Shaney, pushing Aline in front of him toward her father standing over the engineer's body. And then Ben's glance went to Wally who had stopped abruptly by the baggage car.

Codine had no time to wonder at Aline's presence here, and he discounted Shaney in that grim moment of decision.

He pulled Nig broadside and lifted up in stirrups, his rifle settling against his shoulder. Wally's quick snapshot whistled over his head. His own fire spun the little man around and slammed him down, off the roadbed.

Paul Shaney whirled at the crack of the rifle behind him. The shock of Ben's appearance unnerved him. He started to run toward the baggage car, then the pound of the black stallion's hoofs, closing fast on him, jerked him around. He threw his unfired Colt away and raised his hands, stumbling back from that grim-faced rider until his shoulder touched the engine.

Ben rode past Shaney, dismounting on the run. Ira's face appeared briefly in the doorway. His hand spat flame. Ben's Colt chipped wood from the edge of the baggage car door and Flint ducked back inside, cursing.

Codine kept close to the tender. He had his man trapped inside the baggage car, but Flint was still as dangerous as a caged lobo. Harvey had picked up the gun Shaney had thrown away; he was holding it on the cowering bookkeeper. Behind him Aline was starting to run toward Ben.

The bounty hunter waved them back. Sooner or later Flint would have to make a break. But the girl or her father might get hurt by a wild bullet.

"Ira!" Ben's voice had an iron ring to it. "You told me once all you wanted was a gun in your hand! An even break. You talked big that day. I haven't forgotten. I'm giving you that even break — now!"

Inside the car Ira heard that challenge. Backed up against the wall, he considered Codine's offer.

He had always played the long odds. This was his last hand. It was more than bravado that lifted the corners of his mouth in an insolent grin. He didn't care about the money; he had never really cared about money. It was Ben Codine he wanted. And Codine was out there, waiting.

"An even break!" he shouted. "You promise?"

Ben's voice came back to him. "My hands are empty, Ira. I'm waiting!"

Flint took one last look through the baggage door opening, to the brush lying dark and dead against the snow, and the high loom of the hills he had known in his boyhood. He took his look and thrust aside the impulse to step up to that opening with his gun cocked in his hand. He wanted to keep that much of a hole card in this last hand with Death.

Some strange quirk of fairness made him slide his Colt back into holster. Made him take two long strides to the door, and turn to face, insolently, the man waiting off the roadbed.

The bounty hunter's hands were down by his sides, as he had promised, that much Ira Flint saw as he shouted a curse and drew. He fired and fired again even as he jerked to the impact of Ben's bullets. His eyes were wide and riveted to the red bursts of flame centering the rolling cloud of smoke at Ben

Codine's hip. He saw this and his own gun jarred aimlessly. That was the last thing he saw, and Wally's bitter words were the last thing he remembered.

"You'll live to regret it!"

He fell forward out of the car over Radisek's body, and he was dead before he stopped rolling.

Ben turned as Aline, crying, began running toward him. Only then was he aware of the blood on his face. He lifted a hand to touch the shallow gash above his left eye.

Ira Flint had come close!

He turned to meet the running girl, a weariness sagging his shoulders. In the distance he could see a line of horsemen emerging through the ridge cut from town, and the thought came to him that Mido Peters had finally made up his mind.

Later, a frightened Paul Shaney confirmed Ben Codine's story and disclosed his part in it.

Jake Grady paid off his men on schedule. But it was a sober gathering who received the money.

Radisek was dead. The fireman and the engineer of the Special would live, but the engineer would never grip the throttle again.

Ben Codine had supper with the Buskins, a quiet supper. He told them about himself, and why he had not felt he could speak before. They understood.

Aline Buskin walked with him to the tele-graph office. The wire he sent Sheriff Tolliver read:

"Am getting married. Best to you and Kit and the kids. Will be down in the Spring. Want you to meet Aline. Regards,

Ben"

About the Author

PETER B. GERMANO was born the oldest of six children in New Bedford, Massachusetts. During the Great Depression, he had to go to work before completing high school. It left him with a powerful drive to continue his formal education later in life, finally earning a Master's degree from Loyola University in Los Angeles in 1970. He sold his first Western story to A. A. Wyn's Ace Publishing magazine group when he was twenty years old. In the same issue of *Sure-Fire Western* (1/39) Germano had two stories, one by Peter Germano and the other by Barry Cord. He came to prefer the Barry Cord name for his Western fiction. When the Second World War came, he joined the U.S. Marine Corps. Following the war he would be called back to active duty, again as a combat correspondent, during the Korean conflict. In 1948 Germano began publishing a series of Western novels as Barry Cord notable for their complex plots while the scenes themselves are simply set, with a minimum of description and quick character sketches employed to establish a wide assortment of very different personalities. The pacing, which often seems swift due to the adept use of a parallel plot structure (narrating a story from several different viewpoints), is combined in these novels with atmospheric descriptions of weather and terrain. *Dry Range* (1955), *The Sagebrush Kid* (1954), *The Iron Trail Killers* (1960), and *Trouble in Peaceful Valley* (1968) are among his best Westerns. "The great southwest . . ." Germano wrote in 1982, "this is the country, and these are the people that gripped my imagination . . . and this is what I have been writing about for forty years. And until I die I shall remain the little New England boy who fell in love with the 'West,' and as a man had the opportunity to see it and live in it."